D0717169

1 3 5 7 9 10 8 6 4 2

Vintage
20 Vauxhall Bridge Road,
London SW1V 2SA

Vintage Classics is part of the Penguin Random House
group of companies whose addresses can be found at
global.penguinrandomhouse.com.

Penguin
Random House
UK

The Elephant Vanishes first published in Great Britain in 1993
by Hamish Hamilton
First published by Vintage in 2003

Blind Woman, Sleeping Willow first published in Great Britain in 2006 by Harvill
Secker
First published by Vintage in 2007

Men Without Women first published in Great Britain in 2017 by Harvill Secker

This short edition published by Vintage in 2017

penguin.co.uk/vintage

A CIP catalogue record for this book is available from the British Library

ISBN 9781784872632

Typeset in 9.5/14.5 pt FreightText Pro
by Jouve (UK), Milton Keynes
Printed and bound by Clays Ltd, St Ives plc

Penguin Random House is committed to a sustainable future for
our business, our readers and our planet. This book is made from
Forest Stewardship Council® certified paper.

Desire

HARUKI MURAKAMI

Translated from the Japanese by Jay Rubin,
Ted Goossen and Philip Gabriel

VINTAGE MINIS

The Second Bakery Attack

I'M STILL NOT SURE I made the right choice when I told my wife about the bakery attack. But then, it might not have been a question of right and wrong. Which is to say that wrong choices can produce right results, and vice versa. I myself have adopted the position that, in fact, *we never choose anything at all*. Things happen. Or not.

If you look at it this way, *it just so happens* that I told my wife about the bakery attack. I hadn't been planning to bring it up – I had forgotten all about it – but it wasn't one of those now-that-you-mention-it kind of things, either.

What reminded me of the bakery attack was an unbearable hunger. It hit just before two o'clock in the morning. We had eaten a light supper at six, crawled into bed at nine-thirty, and gone to sleep. For some reason, we woke up at exactly the same moment. A few minutes later, the pangs struck with the force of the tornado in *The Wizard of Oz*. These were tremendous, overpowering hunger pangs.

Our refrigerator contained not a single item that could

be technically categorized as food. We had a bottle of French dressing, six cans of beer, two shriveled onions, a stick of butter, and a box of refrigerator deodorizer. With only two weeks of married life behind us, we had yet to establish a precise conjugal understanding with regard to the rules of dietary behavior. Let alone anything else.

I had a job in a law firm at the time, and she was doing secretarial work at a design school. I was either twenty-eight or twenty-nine – why can't I remember the exact year we married? – and she was two years and eight months younger. Groceries were the last things on our minds.

We both felt too hungry to go back to sleep, but it hurt just to lie there. On the other hand, we were also too hungry to do anything useful. We got out of bed and drifted into the kitchen, ending up across the table from each other. What could have caused such violent hunger pangs?

We took turns opening the refrigerator door and hoping, but no matter how many times we looked inside, the contents never changed. Beer and onions and butter and dressing and deodorizer. It might have been possible to sauté the onions in the butter, but there was no chance those two shriveled onions could fill our empty stomachs. Onions are meant to be eaten with other things. They are not the kind of food you use to satisfy an appetite.

'Would madame care for some French dressing sautéed in deodorizer?'

I expected her to ignore my attempt at humor, and she

did. 'Let's get in the car and look for an all-night restaur-ant,' I said. 'There must be one on the highway.'

She rejected that suggestion. 'We can't. You're not supposed to go out to eat after midnight.' She was old-fashioned that way.

I breathed once and said, 'I guess not.'

Whenever my wife expressed such an opinion (or the-sis) back then, it reverberated in my ears with the authority of a revelation. Maybe that's what happens with newly-weds, I don't know. But when she said this to me, I began to think that this was a special hunger, not one that could be satisfied through the mere expedient of taking it to an all-night restaurant on the highway.

A special kind of hunger. And what might that be?

I can present it here in the form of a cinematic image.

One, I am in a little boat, floating on a quiet sea. *Two*, I look down, and in the water I see the peak of a volcano thrusting up from the ocean floor. *Three*, the peak seems pretty close to the water's surface, but just how close I cannot tell. *Four*, this is because the hypertransparency of the water interferes with the perception of distance.

This is a fairly accurate description of the image that arose in my mind during the two or three seconds between the time my wife said she refused to go to an all-night res-taurant and I agreed with my 'I guess not.' Not being Sigmund Freud, I was, of course, unable to analyze with any precision what this image signified, but I knew intui-tively that it was a revelation. Which is why – the almost grotesque intensity of my hunger notwithstanding – I all but automatically agreed with her thesis (or declaration).

We did the only thing we could do: opened the beer. It was a lot better than eating those onions. She didn't like beer much, so we divided the cans, two for her, four for me. While I was drinking the first one, she searched the kitchen shelves like a squirrel in November. Eventually, she turned up a package that had four butter cookies in the bottom. They were leftovers, soft and soggy, but we each ate two, savoring every crumb.

It was no use. Upon this hunger of ours, as vast and boundless as the Sinai Peninsula, the butter cookies and beer left not a trace.

Time oozed through the dark like a lead weight in a fish's gut. I read the print on the aluminum beer cans. I stared at my watch. I looked at the refrigerator door. I turned the pages of yesterday's paper. I used the edge of a postcard to scrape together the cookie crumbs on the tabletop.

'I've never been this hungry in my whole life,' she said. 'I wonder if it has anything to do with being married.'

'Maybe,' I said. 'Or maybe not.'

While she hunted for more fragments of food, I leaned over the edge of my boat and looked down at the peak of the underwater volcano. The clarity of the ocean water all around the boat gave me an unsettled feeling, as if a hollow had opened somewhere behind my solar plexus – a hermetically sealed cavern that had neither entrance nor exit.

Something about this weird sense of absence – this sense of the existential reality of nonexistence – resembled the paralyzing fear you might feel when you climb to the very top of a high steeple. This connection between hunger and acrophobia was a new discovery for me.

Which is when it occurred to me that I had once before had this same kind of experience. My stomach had been just as empty then . . . When? . . . Oh, sure, that was—

'The time of the bakery attack,' I heard myself saying.

'The bakery attack? What are you talking about?'

And so it started.

'I ONCE ATTACKED a bakery. Long time ago. Not a big bakery. Not famous. The bread was nothing special. Not bad, either. One of those ordinary little neighborhood bakeries right in the middle of a block of shops. Some old guy ran it who did everything himself. Baked in the morning, and when he sold out, he closed up for the day.'

'If you were going to attack a bakery, why that one?'

'Well, there was no point in attacking a big bakery. All we wanted was bread, not money. We were attackers, not robbers.'

'We? Who's we?'

'My best friend back then. Ten years ago. We were so broke we couldn't buy toothpaste. Never had enough food. We did some pretty awful things to get our hands on food. The bakery attack was one.'

'I don't get it.' She looked hard at me. Her eyes could

have been searching for a faded star in the morning sky. 'Why didn't you get a job? You could have worked after school. That would have been easier than attacking bakeries.'

'We didn't want to work. We were absolutely clear on that.'

'Well, you're working now, aren't you?'

I nodded and sucked some more beer. Then I rubbed my eyes. A kind of beery mud had oozed into my brain and was struggling with my hunger pangs.

'Times change. People change,' I said. 'Let's go back to bed. We've got to get up early.'

'I'm not sleepy. I want you to tell me about the bakery attack.'

'There's nothing to tell. No action. No excitement.'

'Was it a success?'

I gave up on sleep and ripped open another beer. Once she gets interested in a story, she has to hear it all the way through. That's just the way she is.

'Well, it was kind of a success. And kind of not. We got what we wanted. But as a holdup, it didn't work. The baker gave us the bread before we could take it from him.'

'Free?'

'Not exactly, no. That's the hard part.' I shook my head. 'The baker was a classical-music freak, and when we got there, he was listening to an album of Wagner overtures. So he made us a deal. If we would listen to the record all the way through, we could take as much bread as we liked. I talked it over with my buddy and we figured, Okay. It wouldn't be work in the purest sense of the word, and it wouldn't hurt anybody. So we put our knives back in our bag, pulled up a couple of chairs, and listened to the overtures to *Tannhäuser* and *The Flying Dutchman*.'

'And after that, you got your bread?'

'Right. Most of what he had in the shop. Stuffed it in our bag and took it home. Kept us fed for maybe four or five days.' I took another sip. Like soundless waves from an undersea earthquake, my sleepiness gave my boat a long, slow rocking.

'Of course, we accomplished our mission. We got the bread. But you couldn't say we had committed a crime. It was more of an exchange. We listened to Wagner with him, and in return, we got our bread. Legally speaking, it was more like a commercial transaction.'

'But listening to Wagner is not work,' she said.

'Oh, no, absolutely not. If the baker had insisted that we wash his dishes or clean his windows or something, we would have turned him down. But he didn't. All he wanted from us was to listen to his Wagner LP from beginning to end. Nobody could have anticipated that. I mean – Wagner? It was like the baker put a curse on us. Now that I think of it, we should have refused. We should have threatened him with our knives and taken the damn bread. Then there wouldn't have been any problem.'

'You had a problem?'

I rubbed my eyes again.

'Sort of. Nothing you could put your finger on. But things started to change after that. It was kind of a turning point. Like, I went back to the university, and I graduated, and I started working for the firm and studying for the bar exam, and I met you and got married. I never did anything like that again. No more bakery attacks.'

'That's it?'

'Yup, that's all there was to it.' I drank the last of the beer. Now all six cans were gone. Six pull-tabs lay in the ashtray like scales from a mermaid.

Of course, it wasn't true that nothing had happened as a result of the bakery attack. There were plenty of things that you could easily have put your finger on, but I didn't want to talk about them with her.

'So, this friend of yours, what's he doing now?'

'I have no idea. Something happened, some nothing kind of thing, and we stopped hanging around together. I haven't seen him since. I don't know what he's doing.'

For a while, she didn't speak. She probably sensed that I wasn't telling her the whole story. But she wasn't ready to press me on it.

'Still,' she said, 'that's why you two broke up, isn't it? The bakery attack was the direct cause.'

'Maybe so. I guess it was more intense than either of us realized. We talked about the relationship of bread to Wagner for days after that. We kept asking ourselves if we had made the right choice. We couldn't decide. Of course, if you look at it sensibly, we *did* make the right choice.

Nobody got hurt. Everybody got what he wanted. The baker – I still can't figure out why he did what he did – but anyway, he succeeded with his Wagner propaganda. And we succeeded in stuffing our faces with bread.

'But even so, we had this feeling that we had made a terrible mistake. And somehow, this mistake has just stayed there, unresolved, casting a dark shadow on our lives. That's why I used the word "curse." It's true. It was like a curse.'

'Do you think you still have it?'

I took the six pull-tabs from the ashtray and arranged them into an aluminum ring the size of a bracelet.

'Who knows? I don't know. I bet the world is full of curses. It's hard to tell which curse makes any one thing go wrong.'

'That's not true.' She looked right at me. 'You can tell, if you think about it. And unless you, yourself, personally break the curse, it'll stick with you like a toothache. It'll torture you till you die. And not just you. Me, too.'

'You?'

'Well, I'm your best friend now, aren't I? Why do you think we're both so hungry? I never, ever, once in my life felt a hunger like this until I married you. Don't you think it's abnormal? Your curse is working on me, too.'

I nodded. Then I broke up the ring of pull-tabs and put them back in the ashtray. I didn't know if she was right, but I did feel she was onto something.

The feeling of starvation was back, stronger than ever,

I never, ever, once in my
life felt a hunger like
this until I married you

and it was giving me a deep headache. Every twinge of my stomach was being transmitted to the core of my head by a clutch cable, as if my insides were equipped with all kinds of complicated machinery.

I took another look at my undersea volcano. The water was even clearer than before – much clearer. Unless you looked closely, you might not even notice it was there. It felt as though the boat were floating in midair, with absolutely nothing to support it. I could see every little pebble on the bottom. All I had to do was reach out and touch them.

'We've only been living together for two weeks,' she said, 'but all this time I've been feeling some kind of weird presence.' She looked directly into my eyes and brought her hands together on the tabletop, her fingers interlocking. 'Of course, I didn't know it was a curse until now. This explains everything. You're under a curse.'

'What kind of presence?'

'Like there's this heavy, dusty curtain that hasn't been washed for years, hanging down from the ceiling.'

'Maybe it's not a curse. Maybe it's just me,' I said, and smiled.

She did not smile.

'No, it's not you,' she said.

'Okay, suppose you're right. Suppose it is a curse. What can I do about it?'

'Attack another bakery. Right away. Now. It's the only way.'

'Now?'

'Yes. Now. While you're still hungry. You have to finish what you left unfinished.'

'But it's the middle of the night. Would a bakery be open now?'

'We'll find one. Tokyo's a big city. There must be at least one all-night bakery.'

WE GOT INTO my old Corolla and started drifting around the streets of Tokyo at 2:30 a.m., looking for a bakery. There we were, me clutching the steering wheel, she in the navigator's seat, the two of us scanning the street like hungry eagles in search of prey. Stretched out on the backseat, long and stiff as a dead fish, was a Remington automatic shotgun. Its shells rustled dryly in the pocket of my wife's windbreaker. We had two black ski masks in the glove compartment. Why my wife owned a shotgun, I had no idea. Or ski masks. Neither of us had ever skied. But she didn't explain and I didn't ask. Married life is weird, I felt.

Impeccably equipped, we were nevertheless unable to find an all-night bakery. I drove through the empty streets, from Yoyogi to Shinjuku, on to Yotsuya and Akasaka, Aoyama, Hiroo, Roppongi, Daikanyama, and Shibuya. Late-night Tokyo had all kinds of people and shops, but no bakeries.

Twice we encountered patrol cars. One was huddled at the side of the road, trying to look inconspicuous. The other slowly overtook us and crept past, finally moving off into the distance. Both times I grew damp under the arms, but my wife's concentration never faltered. She was looking for that bakery. Every time she shifted the angle of her body, the shotgun shells in her pocket rustled like buckwheat husks in an old-fashioned pillow.

'Let's forget it,' I said. 'There aren't any bakeries open at this time of night. You've got to plan for this kind of thing or else—'

'Stop the car!'

I slammed on the brakes.

'This is the place,' she said.

The shops along the street had their shutters rolled down, forming dark, silent walls on either side. A barbershop sign hung in the dark like a twisted, chilling glass eye. There was a bright McDonald's hamburger sign some two hundred yards ahead, but nothing else.

'I don't see any bakery,' I said.

Without a word, she opened the glove compartment and pulled out a roll of cloth-backed tape. Holding this, she stepped out of the car. I got out my side. Kneeling at the front end, she tore off a length of tape and covered the numbers on the license plate. Then she went around to the back and did the same. There was a practiced efficiency to her movements. I stood on the curb staring at her.

'We're going to take that McDonald's,' she said, as coolly as if she were announcing what we would have for dinner.

'McDonald's is not a bakery,' I pointed out to her.

'It's *like* a bakery,' she said. 'Sometimes you have to compromise. Let's go.'

I drove to the McDonald's and parked in the lot. She handed me the blanket-wrapped shotgun.

'I've never fired a gun in my life,' I protested.

'You don't have to fire it. Just hold it. Okay? Do as I say. We walk right in, and as soon as they say "Welcome to McDonald's," we slip on our masks. Got that?'

'Sure, but—'

'Then you shove the gun in their faces and make all the workers and customers get together. Fast. I'll do the rest.'

'But—'

'How many hamburgers do you think we'll need? Thirty?'

'I guess so.' With a sigh, I took the shotgun and rolled back the blanket a little. The thing was as heavy as a sand-bag and as black as a dark night.

'Do we really have to do this?' I asked, half to her and half to myself.

'Of course we do.'

Wearing a McDonald's hat, the girl behind the counter flashed me a McDonald's smile and said, 'Welcome to McDonald's.' I hadn't thought that girls would work at McDonald's late at night, so the sight of her confused me for a second. But only for a second. I caught myself and pulled on the mask. Confronted with this suddenly masked duo, the girl gaped at us.

Obviously, the McDonald's hospitality manual said

nothing about how to deal with a situation like this. She had been starting to form the phrase that comes after 'Welcome to McDonald's,' but her mouth seemed to stiffen and the words wouldn't come out. Even so, like a crescent moon in the dawn sky, the hint of a professional smile lingered at the edges of her lips.

As quickly as I could manage, I unwrapped the shotgun and aimed it in the direction of the tables, but the only customers there were a young couple – students, probably – and they were facedown on the plastic table, sound asleep. Their two heads and two strawberry-milkshake cups were aligned on the table like an avant-garde sculpture. They slept the sleep of the dead. They didn't look likely to obstruct our operation, so I swung my shotgun back toward the counter.

All together, there were three McDonald's workers. The girl at the counter, the manager – a guy with a pale, egg-shaped face, probably in his late twenties – and a student type in the kitchen – a thin shadow of a guy with nothing on his face that you could read as an expression. They stood together behind the register, staring into the muzzle of my shotgun like tourists peering down an Incan well. No one screamed, and no one made a threatening move. The gun was so heavy I had to rest the barrel on top of the cash register, my finger on the trigger.

'I'll give you the money,' said the manager, his voice hoarse. 'They collected it at eleven, so we don't have too much, but you can have everything. We're insured.'

'Lower the front shutter and turn off the sign,' said my wife.

'Wait a minute,' said the manager. 'I can't do that. I'll be held responsible if I close up without permission.'

My wife repeated her order, slowly. He seemed torn.

'You'd better do what she says,' I warned him.

He looked at the muzzle of the gun atop the register, then at my wife, and then back at the gun. He finally resigned himself to the inevitable. He turned off the sign and hit a switch on an electrical panel that lowered the shutter. I kept my eye on him, worried that he might hit a burglar alarm, but apparently McDonald's don't have burglar alarms. Maybe it had never occurred to anybody to attack one.

The front shutter made a huge racket when it closed, like an empty bucket being smashed with a baseball bat, but the couple sleeping at their table was still out cold. Talk about a sound sleep: I hadn't seen anything like that in years.

'Thirty Big Macs. For takeout,' said my wife.

'Let me just give you the money,' pleaded the manager. 'I'll give you more than you need. You can go buy food somewhere else. This is going to mess up my accounts and—'

'You'd better do what she says,' I said again.

The three of them went into the kitchen area together and started making the thirty Big Macs. The student grilled the burgers, the manager put them in buns, and the girl wrapped them up. Nobody said a word.

I leaned against a big refrigerator, aiming the gun toward the griddle. The meat patties were lined up on the griddle like brown polka dots, sizzling. The sweet smell of grilling meat burrowed into every pore of my body like a swarm of microscopic bugs, dissolving into my blood and circulating to the farthest corners, then massing together inside my hermetically sealed hunger cavern, clinging to its pink walls.

A pile of white-wrapped burgers was growing nearby. I wanted to grab and tear into them, but I could not be certain that such an act would be consistent with our objective. I had to wait. In the hot kitchen area, I started sweating under my ski mask.

The McDonald's people sneaked glances at the muzzle of the shotgun. I scratched my ears with the little finger of my left hand. My ears always get itchy when I'm nervous. Jabbing my finger into an ear through the wool, I was making the gun barrel wobble up and down, which seemed to bother them. It couldn't have gone off accidentally, because I had the safety on, but they didn't know that and I wasn't about to tell them.

My wife counted the finished hamburgers and put them into two small shopping bags, fifteen burgers to a bag.

'Why do you have to do this?' the girl asked me. 'Why don't you just take the money and buy something you like? What's the good of eating thirty Big Macs?'

I shook my head.

My wife explained, 'We're sorry, really. But there

weren't any bakeries open. If there had been, we would have attacked a bakery.'

That seemed to satisfy them. At least they didn't ask any more questions. Then my wife ordered two large Cokes from the girl and paid for them.

'We're stealing bread, nothing else,' she said. The girl responded with a complicated head movement, sort of like nodding and sort of like shaking. She was probably trying to do both at the same time. I thought I had some idea how she felt.

My wife then pulled a ball of twine from her pocket – she came equipped – and tied the three to a post as expertly as if she were sewing on buttons. She asked if the cord hurt, or if anyone wanted to go to the toilet, but no one said a word. I wrapped the gun in the blanket, she picked up the shopping bags, and out we went. The customers at the table were still asleep, like a couple of deep-sea fish. What would it have taken to rouse them from a sleep so deep?

We drove for a half hour, found an empty parking lot by a building, and pulled in. There we ate hamburgers and drank our Cokes. I sent six Big Macs down to the cavern of my stomach, and she ate four. That left twenty Big Macs in the back seat. Our hunger – that hunger that had felt as if it could go on forever – vanished as the dawn was breaking. The first light of the sun dyed the building's filthy walls purple and made a giant SONY BETA ad tower glow with painful intensity. Soon the whine of highway truck tires was joined by the chirping of birds. The American

Armed Forces radio was playing cowboy music. We shared a cigarette. Afterward, she rested her head on my shoulder.

'Still, was it really necessary for us to do this?' I asked.

'Of course it was!' With one deep sigh, she fell asleep against me. She felt as soft and as light as a kitten.

Alone now, I leaned over the edge of my boat and looked down to the bottom of the sea. The volcano was gone. The water's calm surface reflected the blue of the sky. Little waves – like silk pajamas fluttering in a breeze – lapped against the side of the boat. There was nothing else.

I stretched out in the bottom of the boat and closed my eyes, waiting for the rising tide to carry me where I belonged.

—*translated by Jay Rubin*

On Seeing the 100% Perfect Girl One Beautiful April Morning

ONE BEAUTIFUL APRIL MORNING, on a narrow side street in Tokyo's fashionable Harajuku neighborhood, I walk past the 100% perfect girl.

Tell you the truth, she's not that good-looking. She doesn't stand out in any way. Her clothes are nothing special. The back of her hair is still bent out of shape from sleep. She isn't young, either—must be near thirty, not even close to a "girl," properly speaking. But still, I know from fifty yards away: She's the 100% perfect girl for me. The moment I see her, there's a rumbling in my chest, and my mouth is as dry as a desert.

Maybe you have your own particular favorite type of girl—one with slim ankles, say, or big eyes, or graceful fingers, or you're drawn for no good reason to girls who take their time with every meal. I have my own preferences, of course. Sometimes in a restaurant I'll catch myself staring at the girl at the table next to mine because I like the shape of her nose.

But no one can insist that his 100% perfect girl correspond to some preconceived type. Much as I like noses, I can't recall the shape of hers – or even if she had one. All I can remember for sure is that she was no great beauty. It's weird.

'Yesterday on the street I passed the 100% perfect girl,' I tell someone.

'Yeah?' he says. 'Good-looking?'

'Not really.'

'Your favorite type, then?'

'I don't know. I can't seem to remember anything about her – the shape of her eyes or the size of her breasts.'

'Strange.'

'Yeah. Strange.'

'So anyhow,' he says, already bored, 'what did you do? Talk to her? Follow her?'

'Nah. Just passed her on the street.'

She's walking east to west, and I west to east. It's a really nice April morning.

Wish I could talk to her. Half an hour would be plenty: just ask her about herself, tell her about myself, and – what I'd really like to do – explain to her the complexities of fate that have led to our passing each other on a side street in Harajuku on a beautiful April morning in 1981. This was something sure to be crammed full of warm secrets, like an antique clock built when peace filled the world.

After talking, we'd have lunch somewhere, maybe see a Woody Allen movie, stop by a hotel bar for cocktails. With any kind of luck, we might end up in bed.

Potentiality knocks on the door of my heart.

Now the distance between us has narrowed to fifteen yards.

How can I approach her? What should I say?

'Good morning, miss. Do you think you could spare half an hour for a little conversation?'

Ridiculous. I'd sound like an insurance salesman.

'Pardon me, but would you happen to know if there is an all-night cleaners in the neighborhood?'

No, this is just as ridiculous. I'm not carrying any laundry, for one thing. Who's going to buy a line like that?

Maybe the simple truth would do. 'Good morning. You are the 100% perfect girl for me.'

No, she wouldn't believe it. Or even if she did, she might not want to talk to me. Sorry, she could say, I might be the 100% perfect girl for you, but you're not the 100% perfect boy for me. It could happen. And if I found myself in that situation, I'd probably go to pieces. I'd never recover from the shock. I'm thirty-two, and that's what growing older is all about.

We pass in front of a flower shop. A small, warm air mass touches my skin. The asphalt is damp, and I catch the scent of roses. I can't bring myself to speak to her. She wears a white sweater, and in her right hand she holds a crisp white envelope lacking only a stamp. So: She's written somebody a letter, maybe spent the whole night writing, to judge from the sleepy look in her eyes. The envelope could contain every secret she's ever had.

I take a few more strides and turn: She's lost in the crowd.

Now, of course, I know exactly what I should have said to her. It would have been a long speech, though, far too long for me to have delivered it properly. The ideas I come up with are never very practical.

Oh, well. It would have started 'Once upon a time' and ended 'A sad story, don't you think?'

Once upon a time, there lived a boy and a girl. The boy was eighteen and the girl sixteen. He was not unusually handsome, and she was not especially beautiful. They were just an ordinary lonely boy and an ordinary lonely girl, like all the others. But they believed with their whole hearts that somewhere in the world there lived the 100% perfect boy and the 100% perfect girl for them. Yes, they believed in a miracle. And that miracle actually happened.

One day the two came upon each other on the corner of a street.

'This is amazing,' he said. 'I've been looking for you all my life. You may not believe this, but you're the 100% perfect girl for me.'

'And you,' she said to him, 'are the 100% perfect boy

for me, exactly as I'd pictured you in every detail. It's like a dream.'

They sat on a park bench, held hands, and told each other their stories hour after hour. They were not lonely anymore. They had found and been found by their 100% perfect other. What a wonderful thing it is to find and be found by your 100% perfect other. It's a miracle, a cosmic miracle.

As they sat and talked, however, a tiny, tiny sliver of doubt took root in their hearts: Was it really all right for one's dreams to come true so easily?

And so, when there came a momentary lull in their conversation, the boy said to the girl, 'Let's test ourselves – just once. If we really are each other's 100% perfect lovers, then sometime, somewhere, we will meet again without fail. And when that happens, and we know that we are the 100% perfect ones, we'll marry then and there. What do you think?'

'Yes,' she said, 'that is exactly what we should do.'

And so they parted, she to the east, and he to the west.

The test they had agreed upon, however, was utterly unnecessary. They should never have undertaken it, because they really and truly were each other's 100% perfect lovers, and it was a miracle that they had ever met. But it was impossible for them to know this, young as they were. The cold, indifferent waves of fate proceeded to toss them unmercifully.

One winter, both the boy and the girl came down with

the season's terrible influenza, and after drifting for weeks between life and death they lost all memory of their earlier years. When they awoke, their heads were as empty as the young D. H. Lawrence's piggy bank.

They were two bright, determined young people, however, and through their unremitting efforts they were able to acquire once again the knowledge and feeling that qualified them to return as full-fledged members of society. Heaven be praised, they became truly upstanding citizens who knew how to transfer from one subway line to another, who were fully capable of sending a special-delivery letter at the post office. Indeed, they even experienced love again, sometimes as much as 75% or even 85% love.

Time passed with shocking swiftness, and soon the boy was thirty-two, the girl thirty.

One beautiful April morning, in search of a cup of coffee to start the day, the boy was walking from west to east, while the girl, intending to send a special-delivery letter, was walking from east to west, both along the same narrow street in the Harajuku neighborhood of Tokyo. They passed each other in the very center of the street. The faintest gleam of their lost memories glimmered for the briefest moment in their hearts. Each felt a rumbling in the chest. And they knew:

She is the 100% perfect girl for me.

He is the 100% perfect boy for me.

But the glow of their memories was far too weak, and their thoughts no longer had the clarity of fourteen years earlier. Without a word, they passed each other, disappearing into the crowd. Forever.

A sad story, don't you think?

YES, THAT'S IT, that is what I should have said to her.

—translated by Jay Rubin

Birthday Girl

SHE WAITED ON tables as usual that day, her twentieth birthday. She always worked on Fridays, but if things had gone according to plan that particular Friday, she would have had the night off. The other part-time girl had agreed to switch shifts with her as a matter of course: being screamed at by an angry chef while lugging pumpkin gnocchi and seafood *fritto misto* to customers' tables was no way to spend one's twentieth birthday. But the other girl had aggravated a cold and gone to bed with unstoppable diarrhoea and a fever of 104°, so she ended up working after all at short notice.

She found herself trying to comfort the sick girl, who had called to apologise. 'Don't worry about it,' she said. 'I wasn't going to do anything special anyway, even if it is my twentieth birthday.'

And in fact she was not all that disappointed. One reason was the terrible argument she had had a few days earlier with the boyfriend who was supposed to be with her that night. They had been going together since school. The argument had started from nothing much, but it had taken an unexpected turn for the worse until it became a long and bitter shouting match – one bad enough, she was pretty sure, to have snapped their long-standing ties once and for all. Something inside her had turned rock hard and died. He had not called her since the blow-up, and she was not going to call him.

Her workplace was one of the better-known Italian restaurants in the chic Roppongi district of Tokyo. It had been in business since the late sixties, and while its cuisine was hardly cutting edge, its high reputation was fully justified. It had many regular customers and they were never disappointed. The dining room had a calm, relaxed atmosphere without a hint of pushiness. Rather than a young crowd, the restaurant drew an older clientele that included some famous stage people and writers.

The two full-time waiters worked six days a week. She and the other part-time waitress were students who took turns working three days each. In addition there was one floor manager and, at the desk, a skinny middle-aged woman who supposedly had been there since the restaurant opened – literally sitting in the one place, it seemed, like some gloomy old character from *Little Dorrit*. She had exactly two functions: to accept payment from the customers and to answer the phone. She spoke only when necessary and always wore the same black dress. There was something cold and hard about her: if you set her afloat on the night-time sea, she would probably sink any boat that happened to ram her.

The floor manager was perhaps in his late forties. Tall and broad-shouldered, his build suggested that he had been a sportsman in his youth, but excess flesh was now beginning to accumulate on his belly and chin. His short, stiff hair was thinning at the crown, and a special ageing bachelor smell clung to him – like newsprint that had been stored in a drawer with cough drops. She had a bachelor uncle who smelled like that.

The manager always wore a black suit, white shirt, and bow tie – not a clip-on bow tie, but the real thing, tied by hand. It was a point of pride for him that he could tie it perfectly without looking in the mirror. He performed his duties adroitly day after day. They consisted of checking the arrival and departure of guests, keeping abreast of the reservation schedule, knowing the names of regular customers, greeting them with a smile, lending a respectful ear to any complaints that might arise, giving expert advice on wines, and overseeing the work of the waiters and the waitresses. It was also his special task to deliver dinner to the room of the restaurant's owner.

'THE OWNER HAD his own room on the sixth floor of the same building where the restaurant was,' she said. 'An apartment, or office or something.'

Somehow she and I had got on to the subject of our twentieth birthdays – what sort of day it had been for each of us. Most people remember the day they turned twenty. Hers had happened more than ten years earlier.

'He never, ever showed his face in the restaurant, though. The only one who saw him was the manager. It was strictly *his* job to deliver the owner's dinner to him. None of the other employees knew what he looked like.'

'So basically, the owner was getting home delivery from his own restaurant.'

'Correct,' she said. 'Every night at eight, the manager had to bring dinner to the owner's room. It was the restaurant's busiest time, so having the manager disappear just then was always a problem for us, but there was no way around it because that was the way it had always been done. They'd load the dinner on to one of those carts that hotels use for room service, the manager would push it into the lift wearing a respectful look on his face, and fifteen minutes later he'd come back empty-handed. Then, an hour later, he'd go up again and bring down the cart with empty plates and glasses. Every day, like clockwork. I thought it was really odd the first time I saw it happen. It was like some kind of religious ritual, you know? But after a while I got used to it, and never gave it another second thought.'

The owner always had chicken. The recipe and the vegetable sides were a little different every day, but the main dish was always chicken. A young chef once told her that he had tried sending up the same exact roast chicken every day for a week just to see what would happen, but there was never any complaint. A chef wants to try different ways of preparing things, of course, and each new chef would challenge himself with every technique for chicken that he could think of. They'd make elegant sauces, they'd try chickens from different suppliers, but none of their efforts had any effect: they might just as well have been throwing pebbles into an empty cave. In the end, every one of them gave up and sent the owner some run-of-the-mill chicken dish every day. That's all that was ever asked of them.

Work started as usual on her twentieth birthday, 17 November. It had been raining on and off since the afternoon, and pouring since early evening. At five o'clock the manager gathered the employees together to explain the day's specials. Servers were required to memorise them word for word and not use crib sheets: veal Milanese, pasta topped with sardines and cabbage, chestnut mousse. Sometimes the manager would play the role of a customer and test them with questions. Then came the employees' meal: waiters in *this* restaurant were not going to have growling stomachs as they took their customers' orders!

The restaurant opened its doors at six o'clock, but guests were slow to arrive because of the downpour, and several reservations were simply cancelled. Women didn't want their dresses ruined by the rain. The manager walked around tightlipped, and the waiters killed time polishing the salt and pepper shakers or chatting with the chef about cooking. She surveyed the dining room with just one couple having their dinner and listened to the harpsichord music flowing discreetly from ceiling speakers. A deep smell of late-autumn rain worked its way from the street.

It was after seven thirty when the manager started feeling sick. He stumbled over to a chair and sat there for a while, pressing his stomach, as if he had just been shot. A greasy sweat clung to his forehead. 'I think I'd better go to the hospital,' he muttered. For him to be taken ill was a wholly uncommon occurrence: he had never missed a day since he started working in the restaurant more than ten years earlier. It was another point of pride for him that he had never been out with illness or injury, but his painful grimace made it clear that he was in a very bad way.

She stepped outside with an umbrella and hailed a taxi. One of the waiters held the manager steady and climbed into the car with him to take him to a nearby hospital. Before ducking into the cab, the manager said to her hoarsely, 'I want you to take a dinner up to room 604 at eight o'clock. All you have to do is ring the bell, say, "Your dinner is here," and leave it.'

'That's room 604, right?' she said.

'At eight o'clock,' he repeated. 'On the dot.' He grimaced again, climbed in, and the taxi took him away.

THE RAIN SHOWED no signs of letting up after the manager had left, and customers arrived at long intervals. No more than one or two tables were occupied at any time, so if the manager and one waiter had to be absent, this was a good time for it to happen. Things could get so busy that it was not unusual even for the full staff to have trouble coping.

When the owner's meal was ready at eight o'clock, she pushed the room-service trolley into the lift and rode up to the sixth floor. It was the standard meal for him: a half-bottle of red wine with the cork loosened, a thermal pot of coffee, a chicken entrée with steamed vegetables, rolls and butter. The heavy aroma of cooked chicken quickly filled the small lift. It mingled with the smell of the rain. Water droplets dotted the lift floor, suggesting that someone with a wet umbrella had recently been aboard.

She pushed the trolley down the corridor, bringing it to a stop in front of the door marked '604'. She double-checked her memory: 604. That was it. She cleared her throat and pressed the doorbell.

There was no answer. She stood there for a good twenty seconds. Just as she was thinking of pressing the bell again, the door opened inward and a skinny old man appeared. He was shorter than she was, by some four or five inches. He had on a dark suit and a tie. Against his white shirt, the tie stood out distinctly, its brownish-yellow colouring not unlike withered leaves. He made a very clean impression, his clothes perfectly pressed, his white hair smoothed down: he looked as though he were about to go out for the night to some sort of gathering. The deep wrinkles that creased his brow made her think of ravines in an aerial photograph.

'Your dinner, sir,' she said in a husky voice, then quietly cleared her throat again. Her voice grew husky whenever she was tense.

'Dinner?'

'Yes, sir. The manager took sick suddenly. I had to take his place today. Your meal, sir.'

'Oh, I see,' the old man said, almost as if talking to himself, his hand still perched on the doorknob. 'Took sick, eh? You don't say.'

'His stomach started to hurt him all of a sudden. He went to the hospital. He thinks he might have appendicitis.'

'Oh, that's not good,' the old man said, running his fingers along the wrinkles of his forehead. 'Not good at all.'

She cleared her throat again. 'Shall I bring your meal in, sir?' she asked.

'Ah yes, of course,' the old man said. 'Yes, of course, if you wish. That's fine with me.'

If I wish? she thought. What a strange way to put it. What am I supposed to wish?

The old man opened the door the rest of the way, and she wheeled the trolley inside. The floor had short grey carpeting with no area for removing shoes. The first room was a large study, as though the apartment was more a workplace than a residence. The window looked out on to the nearby Tokyo Tower, its steel skeleton outlined in lights. A large desk stood by the window, and beside the desk was a compact sofa and love seat. The old man pointed to the plastic laminate coffee table in front of the sofa. She arranged his meal on the table: white napkin and silverware, coffee pot and cup, wine and wine glass, bread and butter, and the plate of chicken and vegetables.

'If you would be kind enough to set the dishes in the hall as usual, sir, I'll come to get them in an hour.'

Her words seemed to snap him out of an appreciative contemplation of his dinner. 'Oh yes, of course. I'll put them in the hall. On the trolley. In an hour. If you wish.'

Yes, she replied inwardly, for the moment that is exactly what I wish. 'Is there anything else I can do for you, sir?'

'No, I don't think so,' he said after a moment's consideration. He was wearing black shoes polished to a high sheen. They were small and chic. He's a stylish dresser, she thought. And he stands very straight for his age.

'Well, then, sir, I'll be getting back to work.'

'No, wait just a moment,' he said.

'Sir?'

'Do you think it might be possible for you to give me five minutes of your time, miss? I have something I'd like to say to you.'

He was so polite in his request that it made her blush. 'I . . . think it should be alright,' she said. 'I mean, if it really is just five minutes.' He was her employer, after all. He was paying her by the hour. It was not a question of her giving or his taking her time. And this old man did not look like a person who would do anything bad to her.

'By the way, how old are you?' the old man asked,

standing by the table with arms folded and looking directly into her eyes.

'I'm twenty now,' she said.

'Twenty *now*,' he repeated, narrowing his eyes as if peering through some kind of crack. 'Twenty *now*. As of when?'

'Well, I just turned twenty,' she said. After a moment's hesitation, she added, 'Today is my birthday, sir.'

'I *see*,' he said, rubbing his chin as if this explained a great deal for him. 'Today, is it? Today is your twentieth birthday?'

She nodded.

'Your life in this world began exactly twenty years ago today.'

'Yes, sir,' she said, 'that is so.'

'I see, I see,' he said. 'That's wonderful. Well, then, happy birthday.'

'Thank you very much,' she said, and then it dawned on her that this was the very first time all day that anyone had wished her a happy birthday. Of course, if her parents had called from Oita, she might find a message from them on her answering machine when she got home from work.

'Well, well, this is certainly a cause for celebration,' he said. 'How about a little toast? We can drink this red wine.'

'Thank you, sir, but I couldn't. I'm working now.'

'Oh, what's the harm in a little sip? No one's going to blame you if I say it's alright. Just a token drink to celebrate.'

The old man slid the cork from the bottle and dribbled a little wine into his glass for her. Then he took an ordinary drinking glass from a glass-doored cabinet and poured some wine for himself.

'Happy birthday,' he said. 'May you live a rich and fruitful life, and may there be nothing to cast dark shadows on it.'

They clinked glasses.

May there be nothing to cast dark shadows on it: she silently repeated his remark to herself. Why had he chosen such unusual words for her birthday toast?

'Your twentieth birthday comes only once in a lifetime, young lady. It's an irreplaceable day.'

'Yes, sir, I know,' she said, taking one cautious sip of wine.

'And here, on your special day, you have taken the trouble to deliver my dinner to me like a kind-hearted fairy.'

'Just doing my job, sir.'

'But still,' the old man said with a few quick shakes of the head. 'But still, lovely young miss.'

The old man sat down in the leather chair by his desk and motioned her to the sofa. She lowered herself gingerly on to the edge of the seat, with the wine glass still in her hand. Knees aligned, she tugged at her skirt, clearing her throat again. She saw raindrops tracing lines down the window pane. The room was strangely quiet.

'Today just happens to be your twentieth birthday, and on top of that you have brought me this wonderful warm meal,' the old man said as if reconfirming the situation. Then he set his glass on the desktop with a little thump. 'This has to be some kind of special convergence, don't you think?'

Not quite convinced, she managed a nod.

'Which is why,' he said, touching the knot of his withered-leaf-coloured necktie, 'I feel it is important for me to give you a birthday present. A special birthday calls for a special commemorative gift.'

Flustered, she shook her head and said, 'No, please, sir, don't give it a second thought. All I did was bring your meal the way they ordered me to.'

The old man raised both hands, palms towards her. 'No, miss, don't *you* give it a second thought. The kind of "present" I have in mind is not something tangible, not something with a price tag. To put it simply –' he placed his hands on the desk and took one long, slow breath – 'what I would like to do for a lovely young fairy such as you is to grant a wish you might have, to make your wish come true. Anything. Anything at all that you wish for – assuming that you *do* have such a wish.'

'A wish?' she asked, her throat dry.

'Something you would like to have happen, miss. If you have a wish – one wish, I'll make it come true. That is the kind of birthday present I can give you. But you had better think about it very carefully because I can grant you only one.' He raised a finger. 'Just one. You can't change your mind afterwards and take it back.'

She was at a loss for words. One wish? Whipped by the wind, raindrops tapped unevenly at the window pane. As long as she remained silent, the old man looked into her eyes, saying nothing. Time marked its irregular pulse in her ears.

'I have to wish for something, and it will be granted?'

Instead of answering her question, the old man – hands still side by side on the desk – just smiled. He did it in the most natural and amiable way.

'Do you *have* a wish, miss – or not?' he asked gently.

'THIS REALLY DID happen,' she said, looking straight at me. 'I'm not making it up.'

'Of course not,' I said. She was not the sort of person to invent some goofy story out of thin air. 'So . . . did you make a wish?'

She went on looking at me for a while, then released a tiny sigh. 'Don't get me wrong,' she said. 'I wasn't taking him one hundred per cent seriously myself. I mean, at twenty you're not exactly living in a fairy-tale world any more. If this was his idea of a joke, though, I had to hand it to him for coming up with it on the spot. He was a dapper old fellow with a twinkle in his eye, so I decided to play along with him. It *was* my twentieth birthday, after all: I reckoned I ought to have *something* not-so-ordinary happen to me that day. It wasn't a question of believing or not believing.'

I nodded without saying anything.

'Do you *have* a wish, miss – or not?' he asked gently

'You can understand how I felt, I'm sure. My twentieth birthday was coming to an end without anything special happening, nobody wishing me a happy birthday, and all I'm doing is carrying tortellini with anchovy sauce to people's tables.'

I nodded again. 'Don't worry,' I said. 'I understand.'

'So I made a wish.'

THE OLD MAN kept his gaze fixed on her, saying nothing, hands still on the desk. Also on the desk were several thick folders that might have been account books, plus writing implements, a calendar and a lamp with a green shade. Lying among them, his small hands looked like another set of desktop furnishings. The rain continued to beat against the window, the lights of Tokyo Tower filtering through the shattered drops.

The wrinkles on the old man's forehead deepened slightly. 'That is your wish?'

'Yes,' she said. 'That is my wish.'

'A bit unusual for a girl your age,' he said. 'I was expecting something different.'

'If it's no good, I'll wish for something else,' she said, clearing her throat. 'I don't mind. I'll think of something else.'

'No, no,' the old man said, raising his hands and waving them like flags. 'There's nothing wrong with it, not at all. It's just a little surprising, miss. Don't you have something else? For example, you want to be prettier, or smarter, or rich: you're OK with not wishing for something like that – something an ordinary girl would ask for?'

She took some moments to search for the right words. The old man just waited, saying nothing, his hands at rest together on the desk again.

'Of course I'd like to be prettier or smarter or rich. But I really can't imagine what would happen to me if any of those things came true. They might be more than I could handle. I still don't really know what life is all about. I don't know how it *works*.'

'I see,' the old man said, intertwining his fingers and separating them again. 'I see.'

'So, is my wish OK?'

'Of course,' he said. 'Of course. It's no trouble at all for me.'

The old man suddenly fixed his eyes on a spot in the air. The wrinkles of his forehead deepened: they might have been the wrinkles of his brain itself as it concentrated on his thoughts. He seemed to be staring at something – perhaps all-but-invisible bits of down – floating in the air. He opened his arms wide, lifted himself slightly from his chair, and whipped his palms together with a dry smack. Settling in the chair again, he slowly ran his fingertips along the wrinkles of his brow as if to soften them, and then turned to her with a gentle smile.

'That did it,' he said. 'Your wish has been granted.'

'Already?'

'Yes, it was no trouble at all. Your wish has been granted,

lovely miss. Happy birthday. You may go back to work now. Don't worry, I'll put the trolley in the hall.'

She took the lift down to the restaurant. Empty-handed now, she felt almost disturbingly light, as though she were walking on some sort of mysterious fluff.

'Are you OK? You look spaced out,' the younger waiter said to her.

She gave him an ambiguous smile and shook her head. 'Oh, really? No, I'm fine.'

'Tell me about the owner. What's he like?'

'I dunno, I didn't get a very good look at him,' she said, cutting the conversation short.

An hour later she went to bring the trolley down. It was out in the corridor, utensils in place. She lifted the lid to find the chicken and vegetables gone. The wine bottle and coffee pot were empty. The door to room 604 stood there, closed and expressionless. She stared at it for a time, feeling it might open at any moment, but it did not open. She brought the trolley down in the lift and wheeled it in to the dishwasher. The chef looked blankly at the plate: empty as always.

'I NEVER SAW the owner again,' she said. 'Not once. The manager turned out to have just an ordinary stomach ache and went back to delivering the owner's meal again himself the next day. I left the job after New Year's, and I've never been back to the place. I don't know, I just felt it was better not to go near there, kind of like a premonition.'

She toyed with a paper coaster, thinking her own thoughts. 'Sometimes I get the feeling that everything that happened to me on my twentieth birthday was some sort of illusion. It's as though something happened to make me think that things happened that never really happened at all. But I know for sure that they *did* happen. I can still bring back vivid images of every piece of furniture and every knick-knack in room 604. What happened to me in there really happened, and it had an important meaning for me, too.'

The two of us kept silent, drinking our drinks and thinking our separate thoughts.

'Do you mind if I ask you one thing?' I asked. 'Or, more precisely, *two* things.'

'Go ahead,' she said. 'I imagine you're going to ask me what I wished for that time. That's the first thing you want to know.'

'But it looks as though you don't want to talk about that.'

'Does it?'

I nodded.

She put the coaster down and narrowed her eyes as if staring at something in the distance. 'You're not supposed to tell anybody what you wished for, you know.'

'I won't try to drag it out of you,' I said. 'I *would* like to know whether or not it came true, though. And also – whatever the wish itself might have been – whether or not you later came to regret what it was you chose to wish for. Were you ever sorry you didn't wish for something else?'

'The answer to the first question is yes and also no. I still have a lot of living left to do, probably. I haven't seen how things are going to work out to the end.'

'So it was a wish that takes time to come true?'

'You could say that. Time is going to play an important role.'

'Like in cooking certain dishes?'

She nodded.

I thought about that for a moment, but the only thing that came to mind was the image of a gigantic pie cooking slowly in an oven at low heat.

'And the answer to my second question?'

'What was that again?'

'Whether you ever regretted your choice of what to wish for.'

A moment of silence followed. The eyes she turned on me seemed to lack any depth. The desiccated shadow of a smile flickered at the corners of her mouth, suggesting a kind of hushed sense of resignation.

'I'm married now,' she said. 'To a CPA three years older than me. And I have two children, a boy and a girl. We have an Irish setter. I drive an Audi, and I play tennis with my girlfriends twice a week. That's the life I'm living now.'

'Sounds pretty good to me,' I said.

'Even if the Audi's bumper has two dents?'

'Hey, bumpers are *made* for denting.'

'That would make a great bumper sticker,' she said. '"Bumpers are for denting."'

I looked at her mouth when she said that.

'What I'm trying to tell you is this,' she said more softly, scratching an earlobe. It was a beautifully shaped earlobe. 'No matter what they wish for, no matter how far they go, people can never be anything but themselves. That's all.'

'There's another good bumper sticker,' I said. '"No matter how far they go, people can never be anything but themselves."'

She laughed aloud, with a real show of pleasure, and the shadow was gone.

She rested her elbow on the bar and looked at me. 'Tell me,' she said. 'What would you have wished for if you had been in my position?'

'On the night of my twentieth birthday, you mean?'

'Uh-huh.'

I took some time to think about that, but I couldn't come up with a single wish.

'I can't think of anything,' I confessed. 'I'm too far away now from my twentieth birthday.'

'You really can't think of anything?'

I nodded.

'Not one thing?'

'Not one thing.'

She looked into my eyes again – straight in – and said, 'That's because you've already *made* your wish.'

———

'BUT YOU HAD better think about it very carefully, my lovely young fairy, because I can grant you only one.' In the darkness somewhere, an old man wearing a withered-leaf-coloured tie raises a finger. 'Just one. You can't change your mind afterwards and take it back.'

—*translated by Jay Rubin*

Samsa in Love

HE WOKE TO DISCOVER that he had undergone a metamorphosis and become Gregor Samsa.

He lay flat on his back on the bed, looking at the ceiling. It took time for his eyes to adjust to the lack of light. The ceiling seemed to be a common, everyday ceiling of the sort one might find anywhere. Once, it had been painted white, or possibly a pale cream. Years of dust and dirt, however, had given it the color of spoiled milk. It had no ornament, no defining characteristic. No argument, no message. It fulfilled its structural role but aspired to nothing further.

There was a tall window on one side of the room, to his left, but its curtain had been removed and thick boards nailed across the frame. An inch or so of space had been left between the horizontal boards, whether on purpose or not wasn't clear; rays of morning sun shone through, casting a row of bright parallel lines on the floor. Why was the window barricaded in such a rough fashion? Was a major storm or tornado in the offing? Or was it to keep someone from getting in? Or to prevent someone (him, perhaps?) from leaving?

Still on his back, he slowly turned his head and examined the rest of the room. He could see no furniture, apart from the bed on which he lay. No chest of drawers, no desk, no chair. No painting, clock, or mirror on the walls. No lamp or light. Nor could he make out any rug or carpet on the floor. Just bare wood. The walls were covered with wallpaper of a complex design, but it was so old and faded that in the weak light it was next to impossible to make out what the design was.

There was a door to his right, on the wall opposite the window. Its brass knob was discolored in places. It appeared that the room had once served as a normal bedroom. Yet now all vestiges of human life had been stripped away. The only thing that remained was his solitary bed in the center. And it had no bedding. No sheets, no coverlet, no pillow. Just an ancient mattress.

Samsa had no idea where he was, or what he should do. All he knew was that he was now a human whose name was Gregor Samsa. And how did he know *that*? Perhaps someone had whispered it in his ear while he lay sleeping? But who had he been before he became Gregor Samsa? *What* had he been?

The moment he began contemplating that question, however, something like a black column of mosquitoes swirled up in his head. The column grew thicker and denser as it moved to a softer part of his brain, buzzing all the way. Samsa decided to stop thinking. Trying to think anything through at this point was too great a burden.

In any case, he had to learn how to move his body. He couldn't lie there staring up at the ceiling forever. The posture left him much too vulnerable. He had no chance of surviving an attack – by predatory birds, for example. As a first step, he tried to move his fingers. There were ten of them, long things affixed to his two hands. Each was equipped with a number of joints, which made synchronizing their movements very complicated. To make matters worse, his body felt numb, as though it were immersed in a sticky, heavy liquid, so that it was difficult to send strength to his extremities.

Nevertheless, after repeated attempts and failures, by closing his eyes and focusing his mind he was able to bring his fingers more under control. Little by little, he was learning how to make them work together. As his fingers became operational, the numbness that had enveloped his body withdrew. In its place – like a dark and sinister reef revealed by a retreating tide – came an excruciating pain.

It took Samsa some time to realize that the pain was hunger. This ravenous desire for food was new to him, or at least he had no memory of experiencing anything like it. It was as if he had not had a bite to eat for a week. As if the center of his body were now a cavernous void. His bones creaked; his muscles clenched; his organs twitched.

Unable to withstand the pain any longer, Samsa put his

elbows on the mattress and, bit by bit, pushed himself up. His spine emitted several low and sickening cracks in the process. My goodness, Samsa thought, how long have I been lying here? His body protested each move. But he struggled through, marshaling his strength, until, at last, he managed to sit up.

Samsa looked down in dismay at his naked body. How ill-formed it was! Worse than ill-formed. It possessed no means of self-defense. Smooth white skin (covered by only a perfunctory amount of hair) with fragile blue blood vessels visible through it; a soft, unprotected belly; ludicrous, impossibly shaped genitals; gangly arms and legs (just two of each!); a scrawny, breakable neck; an enormous, misshapen head with a tangle of stiff hair on its crown; two absurd ears, jutting out like a pair of seashells. *Was this thing really him?* Could a body so preposterous, so easy to destroy (no shell for protection, no weapons for attack), survive in the world? Why hadn't he been turned into a fish? Or a sunflower? A fish or a sunflower made sense. More sense, anyway, than this creature, Gregor Samsa. There was no other way to look at it.

Steeling himself, he lowered his legs over the edge of the bed until the soles of his feet touched the floor. The unexpected cold of the bare wood made him gasp. After several failed attempts that sent him crashing to the floor, at last he was able to balance on his two feet. He stood there, bruised and sore, one hand clutching the frame of the bed for support. His head was inordinately heavy and hard to hold up. Sweat streamed from his armpits, and his genitals shrank from the stress. He had to take several deep breaths before his constricted muscles began to relax.

Once he was used to standing, he had to learn to walk. Walking on two legs amounted to a kind of torture, each movement an exercise in pain. No matter how he looked at it, advancing his right and left legs one after the other was a bizarre proposition that flouted all natural laws, while the precarious distance from his eyes to the ground made him cringe in fear. It took time to learn how to coordinate his hip and knee joints, and even longer to balance their movements. Each time he took a step forward, his knees shook with terror, and he steadied himself against the wall with both hands.

But he knew that he could not remain in this room forever. If he didn't find food, and quickly, his starving belly would consume his own flesh, and he would cease to exist.

HE TOTTERED TOWARD the door, pawing at the wall as he went. The journey seemed to take hours, although he had no way of measuring the time, except by the pain. His movements were awkward, his pace snail-like. He couldn't advance without leaning on something for support. On the street, his best hope would be that people saw him as disabled. Yet, despite the discomfort, with each step he was learning how his joints and muscles worked.

He grasped the doorknob and pulled. It didn't budge. A

push yielded the same result. Next, he turned the knob to the right and pulled. The door opened partway with a slight squeak. It hadn't been locked. He poked his head through the opening and looked out. The hallway was deserted. It was as quiet as the bottom of the ocean. He extended his left leg through the doorway, swung the upper half of his body out, with one hand on the door-frame, and followed with his right leg. He moved slowly down the corridor in his bare feet, hands on the wall.

There were four doors in the hallway, including the one he had just used. All were identical, fashioned of the same dark wood. What, or who, lay beyond them? He longed to open them and find out. Perhaps then he might begin to understand the mysterious circumstances in which he found himself. Or at least discover a clue of some sort. Nevertheless, he passed by each of the doors, making as little noise as possible. The need to fill his belly trumped his curiosity. He had to find something substantial to eat, and quickly.

And now he knew where to find that 'something substantial.'

Just follow the smell, he thought, sniffing. It was the aroma of cooked food, tiny particles that wafted to him through the air. The information gathered by olfactory receptors in his nose was being transmitted to his brain, producing an anticipation so vivid, a craving so violent, that he could feel his innards being slowly twisted, as if by an experienced torturer. Saliva flooded his mouth.

To reach the source of the aroma, however, he would have to go down a steep flight of stairs, seventeen of them. He was having a hard enough time walking on level ground – navigating those steps would be a true nightmare. He grabbed the banister with both hands and began his descent. His skinny ankles felt ready to collapse under his weight, and he almost went tumbling down the steps. When he twisted his body to right himself his bones and muscles shrieked in pain.

And what was on Samsa's mind as he made his way down the staircase? Fish and sunflowers, for the most part. Had I been transformed into a fish or a sunflower, he thought, I could have lived out my life in peace, without our struggling up and down steps like these. Why must I undertake something this perilous and unnatural? It makes no sense – there is no rhyme or reason to it.

When Samsa reached the bottom of the seventeen steps, he pulled himself upright, summoned his remaining strength, and hobbled in the direction of the enticing smell. He crossed the high-ceilinged entrance hall and stepped through the dining room's open doorway. The food was laid out on a large oval table. There were five chairs, but no sign of people. White wisps of steam rose from the serving plates. A glass vase bearing a dozen lilies occupied the center of the table. Four places were set with napkins and cutlery, untouched, by the look of it. It seemed as though people had been sitting down to eat their breakfast a few minutes earlier, when some sudden and unforeseen event sent them all running off.

What had happened? Where had they gone? Or where had they been taken? Would they return to eat their breakfast?

But Samsa had no time to ponder such questions. Falling into the nearest chair, he grabbed whatever food he could reach with his bare hands and stuffed it into his mouth, quite ignoring the knives, spoons, forks, and napkins. He tore bread into pieces and downed it without jam or butter, gobbled fat boiled sausages whole, devoured hard-boiled eggs with such speed that he almost forgot to peel them, scooped up handfuls of still-warm mashed potatoes, and plucked pickles with his fingers. He chewed it all together, and washed the remnants down with water from a jug. Taste was of no consequence. Bland or delicious, spicy or sour—it was all the same to him. What mattered was filling that empty cavern inside him. He ate with total concentration, as if racing against time. He was so fixated on eating that once, as he was licking his fingers, he sank his teeth into them by mistake. Scraps of food flew everywhere, and when a platter fell to the floor and smashed he paid no attention whatsoever.

By the time Samsa had eaten his fill and sat back to catch his breath, almost nothing was left, and the dining table was an awful sight. It looked as if a flock of quarrelsome crows had flown in through an open window, gorged themselves, and flown away again. The only thing untouched was the vase of lilies; had there been less food, he might have devoured them as well. That was how hungry he had been.

HE SAT, DAZED, in his chair for a long while. Hands on the table, he gazed at the lilies through half-closed eyes and took long, slow breaths, while the food he had eaten worked its way through his digestive system, from his esophagus to his intestines. A sense of satiety came over him like a rising tide.

He picked up a metal pot and poured coffee into a white ceramic cup. The pungent fragrance recalled something to him. It did not come directly, however; it arrived in stages. It was a strange feeling, as if he were recollecting the present from the future. As if time had somehow been split in two, so that memory and experience revolved within a closed cycle, each following the other. He poured a liberal amount of cream into his coffee, stirred it with his finger, and drank. Although the coffee had cooled, a slight warmth remained. He held it in his mouth before warily allowing it to trickle down his throat. He found that it calmed him to a degree.

All of a sudden, he felt cold. The intensity of his hunger had blotted out his other senses. Now that he was sated, the morning chill on his skin made him tremble. The fire had gone out. None of the heaters seemed to be turned on. On top of that, he was stark naked – even his feet were bare.

Now that he was sated, the morning chill on his skin made him tremble

He knew that he had to find something to wear. He was too cold like this. Moreover, his lack of clothes was bound to be an issue should someone appear. There might be a knock at the door. Or the people who had been about to sit down to breakfast a short while before might return. Who knew how they would react if they found him in this state?

He understood all this. He did not surmise it, or perceive it in an intellectual way; he knew it, pure and simple. Samsa had no idea where such knowledge came from. Perhaps it was related to those revolving memories he was having.

He stood up from his chair and walked out to the front hall. He was still awkward, but at least he could stand and walk on two legs without clinging to something. There was a wrought iron umbrella stand in the hall that held several walking sticks. He pulled out a black one made of oak to help him move around; just grasping its sturdy handle relaxed and encouraged him. And now he would have a weapon to fight back with should birds attack. He went to the window and looked out through the crack in the lace curtains.

The house faced onto a street. It was not a very big street. Nor were many people on it. Nevertheless, he noted that every person who passed was fully clothed. The clothes were of various colors and styles. Most were men, but there were one or two women as well. The men and women wore different garments. Shoes of stiff leather covered their feet. A few sported brightly polished boots.

He could hear the soles of their footwear clack on the cobblestones. Many of the men and women wore hats. They seemed to think nothing of walking on two legs and keeping their genitals covered. Samsa compared his reflection in the hall's full-length mirror with the people walking outside. The man he saw in the mirror was a shabby, frail-looking creature. His belly was smeared with gravy, and bread crumbs clung to his pubic hair like bits of cotton. He swept the filth away with his hand.

Yes, he thought again, I must find something to cover my body.

He looked out at the street once more, checking for birds. But there were no birds in sight.

The ground floor of the house consisted of the hallway, the dining room, a kitchen, and a living room. As far as he could tell, however, none of those rooms held anything resembling clothes. Which meant that the putting on and taking off of clothing must occur somewhere else. Perhaps in a room on the second floor.

Samsa returned to the staircase and began to climb. He was surprised to discover how much easier it was to go up than to go down. Clutching the railing, he was able to make his way up the seventeen steps at a much faster rate and without undue pain or fear, stopping several times along the way (though never for long) to catch his breath.

One might say that luck was with him, for none of the doors on the second floor were locked. All he had to do was turn the knob and push, and each door swung open. There were four rooms in total, and, apart from the freezing room with the bare floor in which he had woken, all were comfortably furnished. Each had a bed with clean bedding, a dresser, a writing desk, a lamp affixed to the ceiling or the wall, and a rug or a carpet with an intricate pattern. All were tidy and clean. Books were neatly lined up in their cases, and framed oil paintings of landscapes adorned the walls. Each room had a glass vase filled with bright flowers. None had rough boards nailed across the windows. Their windows had lace curtains, through which sunlight poured like a blessing from above. The beds all showed signs of someone's having slept in them. He could see the imprint of heads on pillows.

Samsa found a dressing gown his size in the closet of the largest room. It looked like something he might be able to manage. He hadn't a clue what to do with the other clothes – how to put them on, how to wear them. They were just too complicated: too many buttons, for one thing, and he was unsure how to tell front from back, or top from bottom. Which was supposed to go on the outside, and which underneath? The dressing gown, on the other hand, was simple, practical, and quite free of ornament, the sort of thing he thought he could handle. Its light, soft cloth felt good against his skin, and its color was dark blue. He even turned up a matching pair of slippers.

He pulled the dressing gown over his naked body and, after much trial and error, succeeded in fastening the belt around his waist. He looked in the mirror at himself, clad now in gown and slippers. This was certainly better than walking around naked. Mastering how to wear clothes would require close observation and considerable time. Until then, this gown was the only answer. It wasn't as warm as it might have been, to be sure, but as long as he remained indoors it would stave off the cold. Best of all, he no longer had to worry that his soft skin would be exposed to vicious birds.

WHEN THE DOORBELL rang, Samsa was dozing in the biggest room (and in the biggest bed) in the house. It was warm under the feather quilts, as cozy as if he were sleeping in an egg. He woke from a dream. He couldn't remember it in detail, but it had been pleasant and cheerful. The bell echoing through the house, however, yanked him back to cold reality.

He dragged himself from the bed, fastened his gown, put on his dark blue slippers, grabbed his black walking stick, and, hand on railing, tottered down the stairs. It was far easier than it had been on the first occasion. Still, the danger of falling was ever present. He could not afford to let down his guard. Keeping a close eye on his feet, he picked his way down the stairs one step at a time, as the doorbell continued to ring. Whoever was pushing the buzzer had to be a most impatient and stubborn person.

Walking stick in his left hand, Samsa approached the front door. He twisted the knob to the right and pulled, and the door swung in.

A little woman was standing outside. A very little woman. It was a wonder she was able to reach the buzzer. When he looked more closely, however, he realized that the issue wasn't her size. It was her back, which was bent forward in a perpetual stoop. This made her appear small even though, in fact, her frame was of normal dimensions. She had fastened her hair with a rubber band to prevent it from spilling over her face. The hair was deep chestnut and very abundant. She was dressed in a battered tweed jacket and a full, loose-fitting skirt that covered her ankles. A striped cotton scarf was wrapped around her neck. She wore no hat. Her shoes were of the tall lace-up variety, and she appeared to be in her early twenties. There was still something of the girl about her. Her eyes were big, her nose small, and her lips twisted a little to one side, like a skinny moon. Her dark eyebrows formed two straight lines across her forehead, giving her a skeptical look.

'Is this the Samsa residence?' the woman said, craning her head up to look at him. Then she twisted her body all over. Much the way the earth twists during a violent earthquake.

He was taken aback at first, but pulled himself together. 'Yes,' he said. Since he was Gregor Samsa, this was likely the Samsa residence. At any rate, there could be no harm in saying so.

Yet the woman seemed to find his answer less than satisfying. A slight frown creased her brow. Perhaps she had picked up a note of confusion in his voice.

'So this is *really* the Samsa residence?' she said in a sharp voice. Like an experienced gatekeeper grilling a shabby visitor.

'I am Gregor Samsa,' Samsa said, in as relaxed a tone as possible. Of this, at least, he was sure.

'I hope you're right,' she said, reaching down for a cloth bag at her feet. It was black, and seemed very heavy. Worn through in places, it had doubtless had a number of owners. 'So let's get started.'

She strode into the house without waiting for a reply. Samsa closed the door behind her. She stood there, looking him up and down. It seemed that his gown and slippers had aroused her suspicions.

'I appear to have woken you,' she said, her voice cold.

'That's perfectly all right,' Samsa replied. He could tell by her dark expression that his clothes were a poor fit for the occasion. 'I must apologize for my appearance,' he went on. 'There are reasons . . .'

The woman ignored this. 'So, then?' she said through pursed lips.

'So, then?' Samsa echoed.

'So, then, where is the lock that's causing the problem?' the woman said.

'The lock?'

'The lock that's broken,' she said. Her irritation had been evident from the beginning. 'You asked us to come and repair it.'

'Ah,' Samsa said. 'The broken lock.'

Samsa ransacked his mind. No sooner had he managed to focus on one thing, however, than that black column of mosquitoes rose up again.

'I haven't heard anything in particular about a lock,' he said. 'My guess is it belongs to one of the doors on the second floor.'

The woman glowered at him. 'Your guess?' she said, peering up at his face. Her voice had grown even icier. An eyebrow arched in disbelief. 'One of the doors?' she went on.

Samsa could feel his face flush. His ignorance regarding the lock struck him as most embarrassing. He cleared his throat to speak, but the words did not come.

'Mr Samsa, are your parents in? I think it's better if I talk to them.'

'They seem to have gone out on an errand,' Samsa said.

'An errand?' she said, appalled. 'In the midst of these *troubles*?'

'I really have no idea. When I woke up this morning, everyone was gone,' Samsa said.

'Good grief,' the young woman said. She heaved a long sigh. 'We did tell them that someone would come at this time today.'

'I'm terribly sorry.'

The woman stood there for a moment. Then, slowly, her arched eyebrow descended, and she looked at the black walking stick in Samsa's left hand. 'Are your legs bothering you, Gregor Samsa?'

'Yes, a little,' he prevaricated.

Once again, the woman writhed suddenly. Samsa had no idea what this action meant or what its purpose was. Yet he was drawn by instinct to the complex sequence of movements.

'Well, what's to be done,' the woman said in a tone of resignation. 'Let's take a look at those doors on the second floor. I came over the bridge and all the way across town through this terrible upheaval to get here. Risked my life, in fact. So it wouldn't make much sense to say, "Oh, really, no one is here? I'll come back later," would it?'

This terrible upheaval? Samsa couldn't grasp what she was talking about. What awful change was taking place? But he decided not to ask for details. Better to avoid exposing his ignorance even further.

Back bent, the young woman took the heavy black bag in her right hand and toiled up the stairs, much like a crawling insect. Samsa labored after her, his hand on the railing. Her creeping gait aroused his sympathy – it reminded him of something.

The woman stood at the top of the steps and surveyed the hallway. 'So,' she said, '*one* of these four doors *probably* has a broken lock, right?'

Samsa's face reddened. 'Yes,' he said. 'One of these. It could be the one at the end of the hall on the left, possibly,' he said, faltering. This was the door to the bare room in which he had woken that morning.

'*It could be*,' the woman said in a voice as lifeless as an extinguished bonfire. '*Possibly.*' She turned around to examine Samsa's face.

'Somehow or other,' Samsa said.

The woman sighed again. 'Gregor Samsa,' she said dryly. 'You are a true joy to talk to. Such a rich vocabulary, and you always get to the point.' Then her tone changed. 'But no matter. Let's check the door on the left at the end of the hall first.'

The woman went to the door. She turned the knob back and forth and pushed, and it opened inward. The room was as it had been before: only a bed with a bare mattress that was less than clean. This was the mattress he had woken on that morning as Gregor Samsa. It had been no dream. The floor bare and cold. Boards nailed across the window. The woman must have noticed all this, but she showed no sign of surprise. Her demeanor suggested that similar rooms could be found all over the city.

She squatted down, opened the black bag, pulled out a white flannel cloth, and spread it on the floor. Then she took out a number of tools, which she lined up carefully on the cloth, like an inquisitor displaying the sinister instruments of his trade before some poor martyr.

Selecting a wire of medium thickness, she inserted it into the lock and, with a practiced hand, manipulated it from a variety of angles. Her eyes were narrowed in concentration, her ears alert for the slightest sound. Next, she chose a thinner wire and repeated the process. Her face grew somber, and her mouth twisted into a ruthless shape, like a Chinese sword. She took a large flashlight and, with a black look in her eyes, began to examine the lock in detail.

'Do you have the key for this lock?' she asked Samsa.

'I haven't the slightest idea where the key is,' he answered honestly.

'Ah, Gregor Samsa, sometimes you make me want to die,' she said.

After that, she quite ignored him. She selected a screwdriver from the tools lined up on the cloth and proceeded to remove the lock from the door. Her movements were slow and cautious. She paused from time to time to twist and writhe about as she had before.

While he stood behind her, watching her move in that fashion, Samsa's own body began to respond in a strange way. He was growing hot all over, and his nostrils were flaring. His mouth was so dry that he produced a loud gulp whenever he swallowed. His earlobes itched. And his sexual organ, which had dangled in such a sloppy way until that point, began to stiffen and expand. As it rose, a bulge developed at the front of his gown. He was in the dark, however, as to what that might signify.

Having extracted the lock, the young woman took it to the window to inspect in the sunlight that shone between the boards. She poked it with a thin wire and gave it a hard shake to see how it sounded, her face glum and her lips pursed. Finally, she sighed again and turned to face Samsa.

'The insides are shot,' the woman said. 'It's kaput. This is the one, just like you said.'

'That's good,' Samsa said.

'No, it's not,' the woman said. 'There's no way I can repair it here on the spot. It's a special kind of lock. I'll have to take it back and let my father or one of my older brothers work on it. They may be able to fix it. I'm just an apprentice – I can only handle regular locks.'

'I see,' Samsa said. So this young woman had a father and several brothers. A whole family of locksmiths.

'Actually, one of them was supposed to come today, but because of the commotion going on out there they sent me instead. The city is riddled with checkpoints.' She looked back down at the lock in her hands. 'But how did the lock get broken like this? It's weird. Someone must have gouged out the insides with a special kind of tool. There's no other way to explain it.'

Again she writhed. Her arms rotated as if she were a swimmer practicing a new stroke. He found the action mesmerizing and very exciting.

Samsa made up his mind. 'May I ask you a question?' he said.

'A question?' she said, casting him a dubious glance. 'I can't imagine what, but go ahead.'

'Why do you twist about like that every so often?'

She looked at Samsa with her lips slightly parted. 'Twist about?' She thought for a moment. 'You mean like this?' She demonstrated the motion for him.

'Yes, that's it.'

'My brassiere doesn't fit,' she said dourly. 'That's all.'

'Brassiere?' Samsa said in a dull voice. It was a word he couldn't call up from his memory.

'A brassiere. You know what that is, don't you?' the woman said. 'Or do you find it strange that hunchback women wear brassieres? Do you think it's presumptuous of us?'

'Hunchback?' Samsa said. Yet another word that was sucked into that vast emptiness he carried within. He had no idea what she was talking about. Still, he knew that he should say something.

'No, I don't think so at all,' he mumbled.

'Listen up. We hunchbacks have two breasts, just like other women, and we have to use a brassiere to support them. We can't walk around like cows with our udders swinging.'

'Of course not.' Samsa was lost.

'But brassieres aren't designed for us—they get loose. We're built differently from regular women, right? So we have to twist around every so often to put them back in place. Hunchbacks have more problems than you can imagine. Is that why you've been staring at me from behind? Is that how you get your kicks?'

'No, not at all. I was just curious why you were doing that.'

So, he inferred, a brassiere was an apparatus designed to hold the breasts in place, and a hunchback was a person with this woman's particular build. There was so much in this world that he had to learn.

'Are you sure you're not making fun of me?' the woman asked.

'I'm not making fun of you.'

The woman cocked her head and looked up at Samsa. She could tell that he was speaking the truth – there didn't seem to be any malice in him. He was just a little weak in the head, that was all. Age about thirty. As well as being lame, he seemed to be intellectually challenged. But he was from a good family, and his manners were impeccable. He was nice-looking, too, but thin as a rail with too-big ears and a pasty complexion.

It was then that she noticed the protuberance pushing out the lower part of his gown.

'What the hell is that?' she said stonily. 'What's that *bulge* doing there?'

Samsa looked down at the front of his gown. His organ was really very swollen. He could surmise from her tone that its condition was somehow inappropriate.

'I get it,' she spat out. 'You're wondering what it would be like to fuck a hunchback, aren't you?'

'Fuck?' he said. One more word he couldn't place.

'You imagine that, since a hunchback is bent at the waist, you can just take her from the rear with no problem, right?' the woman said. 'Believe me, there are lots of perverts like you around, who seem to think that we'll let you do what you want because we're hunchbacks. Well, think again, buster. We're not that easy!'

'I'm very confused,' Samsa said. 'If I have displeased you in some way, I am truly sorry. I apologize. Please forgive me. I meant no harm. I've been unwell, and there are so many things I don't understand.'

'All right, I get the picture.' She sighed. 'You're a little *slow*, right? But your wiener is in great shape. Those are the breaks, I guess.'

'I'm sorry,' Samsa said again.

'Forget it.' She relented. 'I've got four no-good brothers at home, and since I was a little girl they've shown me everything. They treat it like a big joke. *Mean* buggers, all of them. So I'm not kidding when I say I know the score.'

She squatted to put her tools back in the bag, wrapping the broken lock in the flannel and gently placing it alongside.

'I'm taking the lock home with me,' she said, standing up. 'Tell your parents. We'll either fix it or replace it. If we have to get a new one, though, it may take some time, things being the way they are. Don't forget to tell them, okay? Do you follow me? Will you remember?'

'I'll tell them,' Samsa said.

She walked slowly down the staircase, Samsa trailing behind. They made quite a study in contrasts: she looked as if she were crawling on all fours, while he tilted backward in a most unnatural way. Yet their pace was identical.

Samsa was trying hard to quell his 'bulge,' but the thing just wouldn't return to its former state. Watching her movements from behind as she descended the stairs made his heart pound. Hot, fresh blood coursed through his veins. The stubborn bulge persisted.

'As I told you before, my father or one of my brothers was supposed to come today,' the woman said when they reached the front door. 'But the streets are crawling with soldiers and tanks. There are checkpoints on all the bridges, and people are being rounded up. That's why the men in my family can't go out. Once you get arrested, there's no telling when you'll return. That's why I was sent. All the way across Prague, alone. "No one will notice a hunchbackgirl," they said.'

'Tanks?' Samsa murmured.

'Yeah, lots of them. Tanks with cannons and machine guns. Your cannon is impressive,' she said, pointing at the bulge beneath his gown, 'but these cannons are bigger and harder, and a lot more lethal. Let's hope everyone in your family makes it back safely. You honestly have no clue where they went, do you?'

Samsa shook his head no. He had no idea.

Samsa decided to take the bull by the horns. 'Would it be possible to meet again?' he said.

The young woman craned her head at Samsa. 'Are you saying you want to see me again?'

'Yes. I want to see you one more time.'

'With your thing sticking out like that?'

Samsa looked down again at the bulge. 'I don't know how to explain it, but that has nothing to do with my feelings. It must be some kind of heart problem.'

'No kidding,' she said, impressed. 'A heart problem, you say. That's an interesting way to look at it. Never heard that one before.'

'You see, it's out of my control.'

'And it has nothing to do with fucking?'

'Fucking isn't on my mind. Really.'

'So let me get this straight. When your thing grows big and hard like that, it's not your mind but your heart that's causing it?'

Samsa nodded in assent.

'Swear to God?' the woman said.

'God,' Samsa echoed. Another word he couldn't remember having heard before. He fell silent.

The woman gave a weary shake of her head. She twisted and turned again to adjust her brassiere. 'Forget it. It seems God left Prague a few days ago. Let's forget about Him.'

'So can I see you again?' Samsa asked.

The girl raised an eyebrow. A new look came over her face – her eyes seemed fixed on some distant and misty landscape. 'You really want to see me again?'

Samsa nodded.

'What would we do?'

'We could talk together.'

'About what?' the woman asked.

'About lots of things.'

'Just talk?'

'There is so much I want to ask you,' Samsa said.

'About what?'

'About this world. About you. About me.'

The young woman thought for a moment. 'So it's not all about you shoving *that* in me?'

'No, not at all,' Samsa said without hesitation. 'I feel like there are so many things we need to talk about. Tanks, for example. And God. And brassieres. And locks.'

Another silence fell over the two of them.

'I don't know,' the woman said at last. She shook her head slowly, but the chill in her voice was less noticeable. 'You're better brought up than me. And I doubt your parents would be thrilled to see their precious son involved with a hunchback from the wrong side of town. Even if that son is lame and a little slow. On top of that, our city is overflowing with foreign tanks and troops. Who knows what lies ahead.'

Samsa certainly had no idea what lay ahead. He was in the dark about everything: the future, of course, but the present and the past as well. What was right, and what was wrong? Just learning how to dress was a riddle.

'At any rate, I'll come back this way in a few days,' the hunchbacked young woman said. 'If we can fix it, I'll bring the lock, and if we can't I'll return it to you anyway. You'll be charged for the service call, of course. If you're here, then we can see each other. Whether we'll be able to have that long talk or not I don't know. But if I were you I'd keep that bulge hidden from your parents. In the real world, you don't get compliments for exposing that kind of thing.'

Samsa nodded. He wasn't at all clear, though, how that kind of thing could be kept out of sight.

'It's strange, isn't it?' the woman said in a pensive voice. 'Everything is blowing up around us, but there are still those who care about a broken lock, and others who are dutiful enough to try to fix it . . . But maybe that's the way it should be. Maybe working on the little things as dutifully and honestly as we can is how we stay sane when the world is falling apart.'

The woman looked up at Samsa's face. She raised one of her eyebrows. 'I don't mean to pry, but what was going on in that room on the second floor? Why did your parents need such a big lock for a room that held nothing but a bed, and why did it bother them so much when the lock got broken? And what about those boards nailed across the window? Was something locked up in there—is that it?'

Samsa shook his head. If someone or something had been shut up in there, it must have been him. But why had that been necessary? He hadn't a clue.

'I guess there's no point in asking you,' the woman said. 'Well, I've got to go. They'll worry about me if I'm late. Pray that I make it across town in one piece. That the soldiers will overlook a poor little hunchbacked girl. That none of them is perverted. We're being fucked over enough as it is.'

'I will pray,' Samsa said. But he had no idea what 'perverted' meant. Or 'pray,' for that matter.

The woman picked up her black bag and, still bent over, headed for the door.

'Will I see you again?' Samsa asked one last time.

'If you think of someone enough, you're sure to meet them again,' she said in parting. This time there was real warmth in her voice.

'Look out for birds,' he called after her. She turned and nodded. Then she walked out to the street.

SAMSA WATCHED THROUGH the crack in the curtains as her hunched form set off across the cobblestones. She moved awkwardly but with surprising speed. He found her every gesture charming. She reminded him of a water strider that had left the water to scamper about on dry land. As far as he could tell, walking the way she did made a lot more sense than wobbling around upright on two legs.

She had not been out of sight long when he noticed that his genitals had returned to their soft and shrunken state. That brief and violent bulge had, at some point, vanished. Now his organ dangled between his legs like an innocent fruit, peaceful and defenseless. His balls rested comfortably in their sac. Readjusting the belt of his gown, he sat down at the dining room table and drank what remained of his cold coffee.

The people who lived here had gone somewhere else. He didn't know who they were, but he imagined that they were his family. Something had happened all of a sudden, and they had left. Perhaps they would never return. What

did 'the world is falling apart' mean? Gregor Samsa had
no idea. Foreign troops, checkpoints, tanks – everything
was wrapped in mystery.

The only thing he knew for certain was that he wanted
to see that hunchbacked girl again. To sit face-to-face and
talk to his heart's content. To unravel the riddles of the
world with her. He wanted to watch from every angle the
way she twisted and writhed when she adjusted her brassiere. If possible, he wanted to run his hands over her body.
To touch her soft skin and feel her warmth with his fingertips. To walk side by side with her up and down the
staircases of the world.

Just thinking about her made him warm inside. No
longer did he wish to be a fish or a sunflower – or anything
else, for that matter. For sure, it was a great inconvenience
to have to walk on two legs and wear clothes and eat with
a knife and fork. There were so many things he didn't
know. Yet had he been a fish or a sunflower, and not a
human being, he might never have experienced this emo-
tion. So he felt.

Samsa sat there for a long time with his eyes closed.
Then, making up his mind, he stood, grabbed his black
walking stick, and headed for the stairs. He would return
to the second floor and figure out the proper way to dress.
For now, at least, that would be his mission.

The world was waiting for him to learn.

—*translated by Ted Goossen*

A Folklore for My Generation:
A Prehistory of Late-Stage Capitalism

I WAS BORN in 1949, entered high school in 1961 and university in 1967. And reached my long-awaited twentieth birthday – my intro into adulthood – during the height of the boisterous slapstick that was the student movement. Which I suppose qualifies me as a typical child of the sixties. So there I was, during the most vulnerable, most immature, and yet most precious period of life, breathing in everything about this live-for-the-moment decade, high on the wildness of it all. There were doors we had to kick in, right in front of us, and you had better believe we kicked them in! With Jim Morrison, the Beatles and Dylan blasting out the soundtrack to our lives.

There was something special about the sixties. That seems true now, in retrospect, but even when I was caught up in the whirlwind of it happening I was convinced of it. But if you asked me to be more specific, to pinpoint what it was about the sixties that was so special, I don't think I could do more than stammer out some trite reply. We were merely observers, getting totally absorbed in some exciting movie, our palms all sweaty, only to find that, after the house lights came on and we left the theatre, the thrilling afterglow that coursed through us ultimately meant nothing whatsoever. Maybe something prevented us from learning a valuable lesson from all this? I don't know. I'm far too close to the period to say.

I'm not boasting about the times I lived through. I'm simply trying to convey what it felt like to live through that age, and the fact that there really *was* something special about it. Yet if I were to try to unpack those times and point out something in particular that was exceptional, I don't know if I could. What I'd come up with if I did such a dissection would be these: the momentum and energy of the times, the tremendous spark of promise. More than anything else, the feeling of inevitable irritation as when you look through the wrong end of a telescope. Heroism and villainy, ecstasy and disillusionment, martyrdom and betrayal, outlines and specialised studies, silence and eloquence, people marking time in the most boring way – they were all there, for sure. Any age has all these. The present does, and so will the future. But in Our Age (to use an exaggerated term) these were more colourful, and you could actually *grasp* them. They were literally lined up on a shelf, right before our very eyes.

Nowadays, if you try to grasp the reality of anything, there's always a whole slew of convoluted extras that come with it: hidden advertising, dubious discount coupons, point cards that stores hand out which you know you should throw away but still hold on to, options that are forced on you before you know what's happening. Back in Our Age, nobody slapped down indecipherable three-volume owner's manuals in front of you. Whatever it was, we just clutched it in our hands and took it straight home – like taking a baby chick home from one of those little night-time stands. Everything was simple, and direct. Cause and effect were good friends back then; thesis and reality hugged each other as if it were the most natural thing in the world. And my guess is that the sixties were the last time that'll ever happen.

A Prehistory of Late-Stage Capitalism – that's my own personal name for that age.

LET ME TELL you a little bit about the young girls back then. And us fellows with our nearly brand new genitals and the wild, joyous, sad sex we had. That's one of my themes here.

Take virginity, for instance – a word that, for some unfathomable reason, always reminds me of a field on a beautiful, sunny spring afternoon. In the sixties, virginity was a much bigger deal than it is today. I'm generalising, of course – I haven't done a survey or anything – but my sense of it is that about 50 per cent of the girls in my generation had lost their virginity by the time they reached twenty. At least among the girls I knew, that seemed to be the case. Which means that about half of the girls, whether they'd made a conscious choice or not, were still virgins.

It strikes me now that most of the girls in my generation – the moderates, you might dub them – whether virgins or not, agonised over the whole issue of sex. They didn't insist that virginity was such a precious thing, nor did they denounce it as some stupid relic of the past. So what actually happened – sorry, but I'm generalising again – was that they went with the flow. It all depended on the circumstances and the partner. Makes sense to me.

So on either side of this silent majority, you had your liberals and your conservatives – the entire spectrum, from girls who practised sex as a kind of indoor sport, to those who were firm believers in remaining pure till they got married. There were guys, too, who were adamant that whoever they married had to be a virgin.

As in every generation, there were all kinds of people, with all kinds of values. But the big difference between the sixties and the decades before and after was that we were convinced that some day all those differences could be overcome.

Peace!

WHAT FOLLOWS IS the story of a fellow I know, a school classmate in Kobe. He was one of those guys who was an all-round star: good marks, good at sports, a natural leader. He was more clean-cut than handsome, I suppose. He had a nice clear voice, and was a good public speaker, even a decent singer. He was always elected class representative, and when our class met as a group he was the one who did the final summary. He wasn't full of original opinions, but in class discussion who expects any originality? There're tons of situations when originality is not what's called for. Most situations, in fact. All we wanted was to get out of there as fast as we could, and we could count on him to wind up the discussion in the time allotted. In that sense, he was a handy sort of fellow to have around.

With him, everything went by the book. If somebody was making a racket in the study hall he'd quietly tell them to simmer down. The guy was basically perfect, but it bothered me that I couldn't work out what was going through his head. Sometimes I felt like tearing his head off his neck and giving it a good shake to see what was rattling around inside. He was very popular with the girls, too. Whenever he popped to his feet in class to say something every girl would gaze at him with a dreamy look of admiration. He was also your go-to guy if you were stuck with a maths problem you couldn't solve. We're talking about someone who was twenty-seven times more popular than me.

If you've ever gone to high school, you know the type I mean. There's somebody like him in every class, the kind that keeps things running smoothly. Years spent in school absorbing training manuals for life have taught me many things, and one of the lessons I came away with was this: like it or not, every group has somebody like him.

Personally, I'm not too fond of the type. For whatever

reason, we just don't click. I much prefer imperfect, more memorable types of people. So with this particular fellow, even though we were in the same class for a year, we never spent time together. The first time we ever had a halfway-decent conversation was after we left school, during the summer holiday when we were first-year students at university. We happened to be taking lessons at the same driving school and talked a few times there. We'd have a cup of tea together while we were waiting. Driving school has got to be one of the most boring places on earth, and if you see a familiar face you jump at it. I don't remember what we talked about, but I know I wasn't left with much of an impression one way or the other.

One other thing I did remember about him was his girl-friend. She was in a different class and was one of a handful of girls who were drop-dead gorgeous. Apart from her stunning looks, she got good results, was good at sports, was kind and a natural leader, and was the one who always summed up class discussions. Every class has a girl like her.

To make a long story short, they were perfect for each other. Mister Clean and Miss Clean. Right out of a tooth-paste commercial.

They were inseparable. During lunch breaks they sat side by side in a corner of the schoolyard, talking. They went home together, too, taking the same train but getting off at different stops. He was on the football team, she was in the English conversation club, and whoever finished earlier than the other would study in the library, waiting so they could go home together. It seemed as though they were together every free moment they had. And they were always talking. I don't know how they could keep from running out of things to say, but somehow they managed it.

We – and by 'we' I mean the guys I hung out with – didn't dislike this couple. We never made fun of them or said bad things about them. In fact, we hardly thought about them at all. They were like the weather, something that was just there, that barely registered on our attention meter. We were too much into our own pursuits, the vital thrilling things the times had to offer. For instance? For instance sex, rock'n'roll, Jean-Luc Godard films, political movements, Kenzaburō Ōe's novels. But chiefly sex.

We were ignorant, conceited kids, of course. We had no idea what life was all about. In the real world there was no such thing as Mister Clean and Miss Clean. They only existed on TV. The kind of illusions we had, then, and the kind of illusions this fellow and his girlfriend had, weren't all that different.

This is their story. It's not a very happy one, and looking back on it now it's hard to locate any lesson in it. But anyway, this is their story, and at the same time *our* story. So it's a kind of folklore that I've collected and now, as a sort of bumbling narrator, will pass on to you.

THE STORY HE told me came out after we had knocked around other topics over some wine, so strictly speaking it might not be altogether true. There are parts I didn't catch, and details I've kind of imagined and woven in. And to protect the real people in it, I've changed some of the facts, though this doesn't have a bearing on the overall story. Still, I think things took place pretty much as set out. I say this because though I might have forgotten some of the details, I distinctly recall the general tone. When you listen to somebody's story and then try to reproduce it in writing, the tone's the main thing. Get the tone right and you have a true story on your hands. Maybe some of the facts aren't quite correct, but that doesn't matter – it actually might elevate the truth factor of the story. Turn this around, and you could say there are stories that are factually accurate yet aren't true at all. Those are the kind of stories you can count on being boring, and even, in some instances, dangerous. You can smell those ones a mile away.

One other thing I need to make clear here is that this former classmate was a lousy storyteller. God might have generously doled out other attributes to the guy, but the ability to relate a story wasn't one of them. (Not that the storyteller's romantic art serves any real purpose in life.) So as he told his story, I could barely stifle a yawn. He'd go off at a tangent, go round in circles, take for ever to remember some of the facts. He'd take a fragment of his story in his hand, frown at it for a while, and once he was convinced he had it right he'd line his facts up one by one on the table. But often this order was wrong. So as a novelist – a story specialist, if you will – I've rearranged these fragments, carefully gluing them together to form what I hope is a coherent narrative.

We happened to run across each other in Lucca, a town in central Italy. I was renting an apartment in Rome at the time. My wife had to go back to Japan, so I was enjoying a leisurely, solitary train trip, first from Venice to Verona, then on to Mantua and Pisa, with a stopover in Lucca. It was my second time there. Lucca's a quiet, pleasant town, and there's a wonderful restaurant on the outskirts of town where they have superb mushroom dishes.

He'd come to Lucca on business, and we just happened to be staying in the same hotel. Small world.

We had dinner together at the restaurant that night. Both of us were travelling alone, and were bored. The older you get, the more boring travelling alone becomes. It's different when you're younger – whether you're alone or not, travelling can be a gas. But as you age, the fun factor declines. Only the first couple of days are enjoyable. After that, the scenery becomes annoying, and people's voices start to grate. There's no escape, for if you close your eyes to block these out, all kinds of unpleasant memories pop up. It gets to be too much trouble to eat in a restaurant, and you find yourself checking your watch over and over as you wait for buses that never seem to arrive. Trying to make yourself understood in a foreign language becomes a total pain.

That's why, when we spotted each other, we breathed a sigh of relief, just like that time we ran across each other at driving school. We sat down at a table near the fireplace, ordered a pricey bottle of red wine, had a full-course mushroom dinner: mushroom hors d'oeuvres, mushroom pasta and *arrosto con funghi*.

It turned out he owned a furniture company that imported European furniture, and was in Europe on a buying trip. You could tell his business was doing well. He didn't boast about it or put on any airs – when he handed me his business card he just said he was running a small company – yet he'd clearly done well for himself. His clothes, the way he spoke, his expression, manner, everything about him made this obvious. He was entirely at home with his worldly success, in a pleasant sort of way.

He told me he'd read all my novels. 'Our way of thinking and goals are very different,' he said, 'but I think it's a wonderful thing to be able to tell stories to other people.'

That made sense. 'If you can do a good job of telling the story,' I added.

At first we talked mainly about our impressions of Italy. How the trains never ran on time, how meals took for ever. I don't remember how it came about, exactly, but by the time we were into our second bottle of wine he'd already started telling his story. And I was listening, making the appropriate signs to show I was keeping abreast. I think he must have wanted to get this off his chest for a long time, but for some reason hadn't. If we hadn't been in a nice little restaurant in a pleasant little town in central Italy, sitting before a fireplace, sipping a mellow 1983

Coltibuono, I seriously doubt if he would have told me the tale. But tell it he did.

'I've always thought I was a boring person,' he began. 'I've never been the type who could just cut loose and have a good time. It was as if I could always sense a boundary around me and I did my best not to step over the line. As though I was following a well-laid-out highway with signs telling me which were the exits, warning me when a bend was coming up, when not to pass. Follow the directions, I reckoned, and life would turn out OK. People praised me for toeing the line, and when I was little I was sure everybody else was doing the same thing as me. But I soon found out that wasn't the case.'

He held his wine glass up to the fire and gazed at it for a time.

'In that sense, my life, at least the beginning stages, went smoothly. But I had no idea what my life meant, and that kind of vague thought only grew stronger the older I got. What did I want out of life? I had no idea! I was good at maths, at English, sports, you name it. My parents always praised me, my teachers always said I was doing fine, and I knew I could get into a good university with no problem. But I had no idea at all what I was aiming at, what I wanted to do. As far as what subject to study, I hadn't a clue. Should I go in for law, engineering or medicine? I knew I could have done well in any one of them, but nothing excited me. So I went along with my parents' and

I could always sense a boundary around me and I did my best not to step over the line

teachers' recommendations and entered the law department at Tokyo University. There was no principle guiding me, really – it's just that everybody said that was the best choice.'

He took another sip of wine. 'Do you remember my girl-friend in school?'

'Was her name Fujisawa?' I said, somehow able to summon up the name. I wasn't entirely sure that was right, but it turned out it was.

He nodded. 'Correct. Yoshiko Fujisawa. Things were good with her, too. I liked her a lot, liked being with her and talking about all kinds of things. I could tell her every-thing I felt, and she understood me. I could go on for ever when I was with her. It was wonderful. I mean, before her, I never had a friend I could really talk to.'

HE AND YOSHIKO were spiritual twins. It was almost uncanny how similar their backgrounds were. As I've said, they were both attractive, smart, natural-born leaders. Form superstars. Both of them were from affluent families, with parents who didn't get along. Both had mothers who were older than their fathers, and fathers who kept a mis-tress and stayed away from home as much as they could. Fear of public opinion kept their parents from divorcing. At home, then, their mothers ruled the roost, and expected their children come top in whatever they did. He and Yoshiko were both popular enough, but never had any real friends. They weren't sure why. Maybe it was because

ordinary, imperfect people always choose similarly imperfect people as friends. At any rate, the two of them were
always lonely, always a bit on edge.

Somehow, though, they hooked up and started going
out. They ate lunch together every day, walked home from
school together. Spent every spare moment with each
other, talking. There was always so much to talk about. On
Sundays they studied together. When it was just the two of
them they could relax the most. Each knew exactly how
the other was feeling. They could talk for ever about the
loneliness they'd experienced, the sense of loss, their
fears, their dreams.

They made out once a week, usually in one of the rooms
of their respective houses. It wasn't hard to be alone; what
with their fathers always gone and their mothers running
errands half the time, their homes were practically deserted. They followed two rules during their make-out
sessions: their clothes had to stay on, and they'd only use
their fingers. They'd passionately make out for ten or fifteen minutes, then sit down together at a desk and study
side by side.

'That's enough. Why don't we study now?' she'd say,
smoothing down the hem of her skirt. They got almost
identical marks, so they made a game out of studying,
competing, for instance, to see who could solve maths
problems the quicker. Studying was never a burden; it was
like second nature to them. It was a lot of fun, he told me.
You might think this is stupid, but we really enjoyed

studying. Maybe only people like the two of us could ever understand how much fun it was.

Not that he was totally happy with their relationship. Something was missing. Actual sex, in other words. 'A sense of being one, physically,' is how he put it. I felt we had to take the next step, he said. I thought if we did, we'd be freer in our relationship, and understand each other better. For me that would have been a completely natural development.

But she saw things differently. Her mouth set, she shook her head slightly. 'I love you so much,' she quietly explained, 'but I want to stay a virgin until I get married.' No matter how much he tried to persuade her, she wouldn't listen.

'I love you, I really do,' she said. 'But those are two different things. I'm not going to change my mind. I'm sorry, but you'll just have to put up with it. You will, if you really love me.'

When she put it that way, he told me, I had to respect her wishes. It was a question of how she wanted to live her life and there wasn't anything I could say about that. To me, whether a girl was a virgin or not didn't matter that much. If I got married and found out my bride wasn't a virgin, I wouldn't care. I'm not a very radical type of person, or a dreamy, romantic sort. But I'm not all that conservative, either. I'm more of a realist, I guess. A girl's virginity just isn't that big a deal. It's much more important that a couple really know each other. But that's only my opinion, and I'm not about to force others to agree. She had her own vision of how her life should be, so I simply had to grin and bear it, and make do with touching her under her clothes. I'm sure you could imagine what this involved.

I can imagine, I said. I have similar memories.

His face reddened a bit and he smiled.

That wasn't so bad, don't get me wrong, but since we never went any further, I never felt relaxed. To me we were always stopping halfway. What I wanted was to be one with her, with nothing coming between us. To possess her, to be possessed. I needed a sign to prove that. Sexual desire was part of it, of course, but that wasn't the main thing. I'm talking about a sense of being one, physically. I'd never once experienced that sense of oneness with a person. I'd always been alone, always feeling tense, stuck behind a wall. I was positive that once we were one, my wall would come crumbling down, and I'd discover who I was, the self I'd only had vague glimpses of.

'But it didn't work out?' I asked him.

'No, it didn't,' he said, and stared for a time at the blazing logs in the fireplace, his eyes strangely dull. 'It never did work out,' he said.

He was seriously thinking of marrying her, and told her so. After we graduate we can get married right away, he told her. We could even get engaged earlier. His words made her very happy, and she beamed a charming smile at him. At the same time, her smile revealed a hint of weariness, of a wiser, more mature person listening to a young person's immature ideas. I can't marry you, she said. I'm going to marry someone a few years older than me, and you're going to marry someone a few years younger. That's the way things are done. Women mature faster than men, and age more quickly. You don't know anything about the world yet. Even if we were to marry straight out of university, it wouldn't work out. We'd never stay as happy as we are now. Of course I love you – I've never loved anyone else. But those are two different things. ('Those are two different things' being her pet saying.) We're still at school, and we've lived sheltered lives. But the world outside isn't like that. It's a big world out there, and we have to get ready for it.

He understood what she was getting at. Compared to other boys his age, he had his feet firmly on the ground. If someone else had been arguing the same point he probably would have agreed. But this was no abstract generalisation. This was his life they were talking about.

I just don't get it, he told her. I love you so much. I want us to be one. This couldn't be clearer to me, or more important. I don't care if it's unrealistic, that's how much I love you.

She shook her head again, as if to tell him it was out of the question. She stroked his hair and said, 'I wonder what either of us knows about love. Our love has never been tested. We've never had to take responsibility for anything. We're still children.'

He couldn't say a thing. It made him miserable that he couldn't smash down the wall around him now. Until then he'd always seen that wall as protecting him, but now it was a barrier, barring his way. A wave of impotence swept over him. I can't do anything any more, he thought. I'm going to be surrounded by this thick wall for ever, never allowed to venture outside. The rest of my insipid, pointless life.

THEIR RELATIONSHIP REMAINED the same until the two of them left school. They'd meet at the library as always, study together, make out with their clothes on. She didn't seem to mind that they never went all the way. She actually seemed to like things left that way, unconsummated. Everybody else imagined that Mister and Miss Clean were both enjoying an uncomplicated youth. But he continued to struggle with his unresolved feelings.

In the spring of 1967, he entered Tokyo University, while she went to a women's university in Kobe. It was definitely a first-rate college, but with her results she could have got into a much better place, even Tokyo University if she'd wanted to. But she didn't think it was necessary, and didn't take the entrance exam. I don't particularly want to study, or get into the Ministry of Finance, she explained. I'm a girl. I'm different from you. You're going to go far. But I want to take a break, and spend the next four years enjoying myself. After I get married, I won't be able to do that again.

He was frankly disappointed. He'd been hoping they'd both go to Tokyo and start their relationship afresh. He pleaded with her to join him, but again she merely shook her head.

He came back from Tokyo for the summer holiday after his first year, and they went on dates almost every day. (That's the summer he and I ran across each other at driving school.) She drove them all around and they continued the same make-out sessions as before. He started, though, to sense that something in their relationship was changing. Reality was invisibly starting to worm its way between them.

It wasn't that there was some obvious change. Actually, the problem was more a *lack* of change. Nothing about her had changed – the way she spoke, her clothes, the topics she chose to talk about, her opinions – they were all as before. Their relationship was like a pendulum gradually grinding to a halt, and he felt out of sync.

Life in Tokyo was lonely. The city was filthy, the food awful, the people uncouth. He thought about her all the time. At night he'd hole up in his room and write letter after letter to her. She wrote back, though not as often. She wrote about all the details of her life, and he devoured her letters. Her letters were what kept him sane. He started smoking and drinking, and cutting classes.

When the summer holiday finally rolled around, though, and he rushed back to Kobe, a lot of things disappointed him. He'd only been away for three months, yet strangely enough his home town struck him now as dusty and lifeless. Discussions with his mother were a total bore. The scenery at home which he'd waxed nostalgic over while he was in Tokyo now seemed to him insipid. Kobe, he discovered, was just a self-satisfied backwater town. He didn't want to talk to anybody, and even going to the barber's he'd gone to since he was a child depressed him. When he took his dog for a walk, the seashore was empty and littered with rubbish.

You'd think that going on dates with Yoshiko would have excited him, but it didn't. Every time they said goodbye, he'd go home and brood. He was still in love with her – that was a given. But it wasn't enough. I have to *do* something, he felt. Passion will get by on its own steam for a time, but it doesn't last for ever. If we don't do something drastic our relationship will reach an impasse, and all the passion will be suffocated out of us.

One day, he decided to raise again the issue of sex that they'd frozen out of their conversations. This will be the last time I bring it up, he decided.

'These last three months in Tokyo I've been thinking about you all the time,' he told her. 'I love you, and my feelings won't change, even if we're away from each other. But being apart so long, all kinds of dark thoughts start to take over. You probably don't understand this, but people are weak when they're alone. I've never been so alone like this in my life. It's awful. So I want something that can bring us closer together. I want to know for sure that we're bound together, even if we're apart.'

But his girlfriend turned him down. She sighed and gently kissed him.

'I'm sorry,' she said, 'but I can't give you my virginity. These are two different things. I'll do anything for you, except that. If you love me, please don't bring that up again.'

He raised the question of their getting married.

'There are girls in my class who are engaged already,' she said. 'Two of them, actually. But their fiancés have jobs. That's what getting engaged involves. Marriage involves responsibility. You become independent and accept another person into your life. If you don't take responsibility you can't gain anything.'

'I can take responsibility,' he declared. 'Listen – I'm going to a top university, and I'm getting good course marks. I can get a job later in any company or government office I want. You name the company and I'll get into it as the top candidate. I can do anything, if I put my mind to it. So what's the problem?'

She closed her eyes, leaned back against the car seat, and didn't say anything for a while. 'I'm scared,' she said. She covered her face with her hands and began to cry. 'I'm so very, very scared. Life is frightening. In a few years, I'll have to go out in the real world and that scares me. Why don't you understand? Why can't you try to understand what I'm feeling? Why do you have to torment me like this?'

He held her close. 'As long as I'm here you don't need to

be afraid,' he said. 'I'm scared, too – as much as you are. But if I'm with you, I am not afraid. As long as we pull together, there's nothing to be afraid of.'

She shook her head again. 'You don't understand. I'm not like you. I'm a woman. You don't get it at all.'

IT WAS POINTLESS for him to say anything more. She cried for a long time, and when she was finished she said the following, rather astonishing thing:

'If . . . we ever broke up, I want you to know I'll always think about you. It's true. I'll never forget you, because I really love you. You're the first person I've ever loved and just being with you makes me happy. You know that. But these are two different things. If you need me to promise you, I will. I *will* sleep with you some day. But not right now. After I marry somebody else, I'll sleep with you. I promise.'

'AT THE TIME I had no idea what she was trying to tell me,' he said, staring at the burning logs in the fireplace. The waiter brought over our entrées and lay a few logs on the fire while he was at it. Sparks crackled up. The middle-aged couple at the table next to us was puzzling over which desserts to order. 'What she said was like a riddle. After I got home I gave a lot of thought to what she'd said, but I just couldn't grasp it at all. Do you understand what she meant?'

'Well, I guess she meant she wanted to stay a virgin

until she got married, and since after she was married there was no reason to be a virgin any more, she wouldn't mind having an affair with you. She was just telling you to wait till then.'

'I suppose that's it. That's the only thing I can think of.'

'It's a unique way of thinking,' I said. 'Logical, though.'

A gentle smile played at his lips. 'You're right. It is logical.'

'She gets married a virgin. And once she's somebody's wife she has an affair. Sounds like some classic French novel. Minus any fancy-dress ball or maids running around.'

'But that's the only practical solution she was able to come up with,' he said.

'A damn shame,' I said.

He looked at me for a while, and then slowly nodded. 'You got that right. I'm glad you understand.' He nodded again. 'Now I can see it that way – now that I'm older. Then, though, I couldn't. I was just a kid. I couldn't grasp all the minute fluctuations of the human heart. So pure shock was my only reaction. Honestly, I was completely floored.'

'I could see that,' I said.

We didn't say anything for a while as we ate.

'As I'm sure you can imagine,' he continued, 'we broke up. Neither of us announced that we were breaking up, it just ended naturally. A very quiet break-up. I think we were too worn out to carry on the relationship. From my perspective, her approach to life was – how should I put it? – not very sincere. No, that's not it . . . What I wanted was for her to have a better life. It disappointed me a little. I didn't want her to get so hung up on virginity or marriage or whatever, but live a more natural, full sort of life.'

'But I don't think she could have acted otherwise,' I said.

He nodded. 'You might be right,' he said, taking a bite of a thick piece of mushroom. 'After a while you become inflexible. You can't bounce back any more. It could have happened to me, too. Ever since we were little, people had been pushing us, expecting us to succeed. And we met their expectations, because we were bright enough to. But your maturity level can't keep pace, and one day you find there's no going back. At least as far as morals goes.'

'That didn't happen to you?' I asked.

'Somehow I was able to overcome it,' he said after giving it some thought. He put his knife and fork down and wiped his mouth with the napkin. 'After we broke up, I started going out with another girl in Tokyo. We lived together for a while. Honestly, she didn't move me as much as Yoshiko did, but I did love her. We really understood each other, and were always up front with each other. She taught me about human beings – how beautiful they can be, the kind of faults they have. I finally made some friends, too, and got interested in politics. I'm not saying my personality changed completely or anything. I was a very practical person, and I still am. I don't write novels, and you don't import furniture. You know what I mean. In university I learned there were lots of realities in the world. It's a huge world, there are lots of different values coexisting, and there's no need to always be the top student. And then I went out into the world.'

'And you've done very well for yourself.'

'I suppose,' he said, and gave a sheepish sigh. He gazed at me as if we were a pair of accomplices. 'Compared to other people of my generation, I make a good living. So on a practical level, yes, I've been successful.'

He fell silent. Knowing he wanted to say more, I sat there, waiting patiently for him to go on.

'I didn't see Yoshiko for a long time after that,' he continued. 'For a long time. I'd graduated and started work at a trading company. I worked there for five years, part of which took me overseas. I was busy every day. Two years after I graduated, I heard that Yoshiko had got married. My mother gave me the news. I didn't ask who she'd married. When I heard the news, the first thought that struck me was: had she been able to keep her virginity until her marriage. After that I felt a little sad. The next day I felt even sadder. I felt that something important was finally over, like a door closed for ever behind me. That's only to be expected, since I loved her. We'd gone out for four years, and I suppose I was still clinging to the hope that we might get married some day. She'd been a huge part of my youth, so it was only natural that I felt sad. But I decided that as long as she was happy, I was OK with it. I honestly felt that way. I was a little – worried about her. There was a part of her that was very fragile.'

The waiter came, removed our plates, and wheeled over the dessert trolley. We both turned down dessert and ordered coffee.

'I got married late, when I was thirty-two. So when Yoshiko called me, I was still single. I was twenty-eight, which makes it more than a decade ago. I'd just left the company I'd been working for and had gone out on my own. I was convinced that the imported furniture market was about to take off, so I borrowed money from my father and started up my own little firm. Despite my confidence, though, things didn't go so well at first. Orders were late, goods went unsold, warehouse fees piled up, there were loans to repay. I was frankly worn out, and starting to lose confidence. This was the hardest time I've ever gone through in my life. And it was exactly during that rough spell that Yoshiko phoned me one day. I don't know how she got my number, but one evening around eight, she called. I knew it was her right away. How could I ever forget that voice? It brought back so many memories. I was feeling pretty down then, and it felt wonderful to hear my old girlfriend's voice again.'

He stared at the blazing logs in the fireplace as if trying to summon up a memory. By this time the restaurant was completely full, loud with the sound of people's voices, laughter, plates clinking. Almost all the guests were locals, it seemed, and they called out to the waiters by first name: *Giuseppe! Paolo!*

'I don't know who she heard it from, but she knew everything about me. How I was still single and had worked abroad. How I'd left my job a year before and started up my own company. She knew it all. Don't worry, she told me, you'll do fine. Just have confidence in yourself. I know you'll be successful. How could you not be? It made me so happy to hear her say that. Her voice was so kind. I can do this, I thought, I *can* make a go of it. Hearing her voice made me regain the confidence I used to have. As long as things stay real, I thought, I know I'm going to make it. I felt as if the world was out there just for me.' He smiled.

'It was my turn then to ask about her life. What kind of person she had married, whether she had children, where she lived. She didn't have any children. Her husband was four years older than her and worked at a TV station. He was a director, she said. He must be very busy, I commented. So busy he doesn't have time to make any children, she replied, and laughed. She lived in Tokyo, in a condo in Shinagawa. I was living in Shiroganedai at the time, so we weren't exactly neighbours but lived pretty close to each other. What a coincidence, I told her. Anyway, that's what we talked about – all the typical things two people who used to go out in school might talk about. Occasionally it felt a bit awkward, but I enjoyed talking to her again. We talked like two old friends who'd said goodbye long ago and who were now walking down two separate paths in life. It had been a long time since I'd spoken so openly, so honestly, to anybody, and we talked for a long, long time. Once we'd said everything there was to say, we were silent. It was a – how should I put it? – a very deep silence. The kind of silence where, if you close your eyes, all sorts of images start to well up in your mind.' He stared for a while at his hands on the table, then raised his head and looked at me. 'I wanted to hang up then, if I could have. Thank her for calling, tell her how much I enjoyed talking to her. You know what I mean?'

'From a practical standpoint that would have been the most realistic thing to do,' I agreed.

'But she didn't hang up. And she invited me to her place. Can you come over? she asked. My husband's on a business trip and I'm by myself and bored. I didn't know what to say, so I said nothing. Nor did she. There was just that silence for a while, and then she said this: I haven't forgotten the promise I made to you.'

'I HAVEN'T FORGOTTEN the promise I made to you,' she said. At first he didn't know what she meant. And then it all came back – her promise to sleep with him after she got married. He'd never considered this a real promise, just a stray thought she'd let slip out in a moment of confusion.

But it hadn't been the result of any confusion on her part. For her it was a promise, a binding agreement she'd entered into.

For a moment he didn't know what to think, no idea

what he should do. He glanced around him, completely at a loss, but discovered no signposts to show him the way. Of course he wanted to sleep with her – that goes without saying. After they broke up, he often imagined what it would be like making love to her. Even when he was with other girls, in the dark he pictured holding her. Not that he'd seen her naked – all he knew about her body was what he'd been able to feel with his hand under her clothes.

He knew full well how dangerous it would be for him to sleep with her at this point. How destructive it could finish up being. He also didn't feel like reawakening what he'd already abandoned back there in the dark. This isn't the right thing for me to do, he knew. There's something unreal about it, something incompatible with who I am.

But of course he agreed to see her. This was, after all, a beautiful fairy tale he might experience only once in life. His gorgeous ex-girlfriend, the one he'd spent his precious youth with, was telling him she wanted to sleep with him, asking him to come over to her house right away – and she lived not far away. Plus there was that secret, legendary promise exchanged a long, long time ago in a deep wood.

He sat there for a while, eyes closed, not speaking. He felt as though he had lost the power of speech.

'Are you still there?' she asked.

'I'm here,' he said. 'OK. I'll be over soon. I should be there in less than a half hour. Tell me your address.'

He wrote down the name of her condo and the

apartment number, and her phone number. He quickly shaved, changed clothes and went out to flag down a taxi.

'IF IT'D BEEN you, what would you have done?' he asked me.

I shook my head. I had no idea what to say.

He laughed and stared at his coffee cup. 'I wish I could have got by without answering, too. But I couldn't. I had to make a decision right then and there. To go or not to go, one or the other. There's no in between. I ended up going to her place. As I knocked on her door, I was thinking how nice it would be if she wasn't at home. But she was there, as beautiful as she used to be. Smelling just as wonderful as I remembered. We had a few drinks and talked, listened to some old records. And then what do you think happened?'

I have no idea, I told him.

'A long time ago, when I was a child, there was a fairy tale I read,' he said, staring at the opposite wall the whole time. 'I don't remember how the story went, but the last line has stayed with me. Probably because that was the first time I'd ever read a fairy tale that had such a strange ending. This is how it ended: "And when it was all over, the king and his retainers burst out laughing." Don't you think that's rather a strange ending?'

'I do,' I said.

'I wish I could remember the plot, but I can't. All I can remember is that strange last line. "And when it was all over, the king and his retainers burst out laughing." What kind of story could it have been?'

We'd finished our coffee by this point.

'We held each other,' he went on, 'but didn't have sex. I didn't take her clothes off. I just touched her with my fingers, just like the old days. I decided that was the best thing to do, and she'd apparently come to the same conclusion. For a long time we sat there, touching each other. That was the only way we could grasp what we were supposed to understand at that time. If this had been long ago, that wouldn't have been the case – we would have had sex, and grown even closer. We might have ended up happy. But we'd already passed that point. That possibility was sealed up, frozen solid. And it would never open up again.'

He turned his empty coffee cup round and round. He did this so long the waiter came over to see if he wanted anything. Finally he let go of the cup, called the waiter back and ordered another espresso.

'I must have stayed at her apartment for about an hour. I don't remember exactly. Any longer and I might have gone a little crazy,' he said and smiled. 'I said goodbye to her and left. This was our final farewell. I knew it, and so did she. The last time I saw her, she was standing in the doorway, arms folded. She seemed about to say something, but didn't. She didn't have to say it out loud – I knew what she was going to say. I felt so empty. So hollow. Sounds struck me as strange, everything looked distorted. I wandered around in a daze, thinking how my life had been utterly pointless. I wanted to turn round, go back to her place and have her. But I couldn't. There was no way I could do that.'

He closed his eyes and shook his head. He drank his second espresso.

'It's pretty embarrassing to say this, but that night I went out and slept with a prostitute. It was the first time in my life I'd paid for sex. And probably the last.'

I stared at my own coffee cup for a while. And thought of how full of myself I used to be. I wanted to try to explain this to him, but didn't think I could.

'When I tell it like this, it sounds like something that happened to somebody else,' he laughed. He was silent for a time, lost in thought. I didn't say anything, either.

'And when it was all over, the king and his retainers burst out laughing,' he finally said. 'That line always comes to me whenever I remember what happened. It's like a conditioned reflex. It seems to me that very sad things always contain an element of the comical.'

As I SAID at the beginning, there's no real moral or lesson to be learned from all this. But this is something that actually happened to him. Something that happened to all of us. That's why when he told me his story, I couldn't laugh. And even now I can't.

—*translated by Philip Gabriel*

© Elena Seibert

HARUKI MURAKAMI was born in Kyoto in 1949, where his parents both taught Japanese literature. Growing up in post-war Japan, Murakami was drawn to Western influences: Franz Kafka, Raymond Carver, Kurt Vonnegut, as well as the liberating rhythms of jazz music. The notion of writing a novel first came to Murakami at the age of 29, while watching a baseball game in Tokyo's Jingu Stadium. He has since written many novels, as well as short stories and non-fiction, including the books *Norwegian Wood*, *The Wind-Up Bird Chronicle*, *Kafka on the Shore*, *1Q84*, *What I Talk About When I Talk About Running*, *Colorless Tsukuru Tazaki and His Years of Pilgrimage* and *Absolutely on Music*.

Murakami's writing is attuned to the deep undercurrents of human desire, with the hunt for satisfaction often taking a turn for the unexpected. In 'The Second Bakery Attack' a young married couple resort to robbery to gratify their hunger, while in 'Samsa in Love' craving offers a gateway into what it means to be fully human. In 'Birthday Girl' Murakami confronts us with the question: what would be our one wish, if we could have it granted.

Murakami has run a marathon a year for over 20 years. He ran his personal best of 3:27 hours in the New York City Marathon in 1991.

RECOMMENDED BOOKS BY HARUKI MURAKAMI:

Blind Willow, Sleeping Woman
The Elephant Vanishes
Men Without Women

Do you want to indulge in your Desire?

Love
JEANETTE WINTERSON

VINTAGE MINIS

Psychedelics
ALDOUS HUXLEY

VINTAGE MINIS

Eating
NIGELLA LAWSON

VINTAGE MINIS

Summer
LAURIE LEE

VINTAGE MINIS

VINTAGE MINIS

The Vintage Minis bring you the world's greatest writers on the experiences that make us human. These stylish, entertaining little books explore the whole spectrum of life – from birth to death, and everything in between. Which means there's something here for everyone, whatever your story.